5 H 5/01

WITHDR

Baldwinsville Public Library
33 East Genesee Street
Baldwinsville, NY 13027-2575

7/5/00

sm 4/02

S0-BJK-673

Reckless Lady

Baldwinsville Public Library
33 East Genesee Street
Baldwinsville, NY 13027-2575

Reckless Lady

RAE FOLEY

Thorndike Press • Chivers Press
Thorndike, Maine USA   Bath, England

This Large Print edition is published by Thorndike Press, USA and by Chivers Press, England. 7|5|00

Published in 2000 in the U.S. by arrangement with Golden West Literary Agency

Published in 2000 in the U.K. by arrangement with Golden West Literary Agency

U.S. Hardcover 0-7862-2581-5 (Candlelight Series Edition)
U.K. Hardcover 0-7540-4188-3 (Chivers Large Print)
U.K. Softcover 0-7540-4189-1 (Camden Large Print)

Copyright © 1973 by Rae Foley

All rights reserved.

The text of this Large Print edition is unabridged.
Other aspects of the book may vary from the original edition.

Set in 16 pt. Plantin by Minnie B. Raven.

Printed in the United States on permanent paper.

British Library Cataloguing-in-Publication Data available

Library of Congress Cataloging-in-Publication Data

Foley, Rae, 1900–
    Reckless lady / Rae Foley.
        p.   cm.
    ISBN 0-7862-2581-5 (lg. print : hc : alk. paper)
    1. Large type books.   I. Title.
  PS3511.O186 R4   2000
    813'.54—dc21   00-028688

Baldwinsville Public Library
33 East Genesee Street
Baldwinsville, NY 13027-2575

Reckless Lady

Baldwinsville Public Library
33 East Genesee Street
Baldwinsville, NY 13027-2575

One

KAY SPAULDING MARRIES AGAIN!

The headline screamed across the top of the newspaper and I stood stock still in the middle of the street staring at it until the strident sound of an automobile horn startled me into leaping for the curb.

In the lobby of the little inn where I was vacationing at Kay's expense and doing some sketching, I read the story. There was a new picture of her, one I had never seen, looking more beautiful than ever before, with a radiance, a glow in her face, that must have been brought there by the new husband.

There was also a picture of the new conquest, Alan Lambert, formerly an actor in Grade B westerns, and now doing a talk show on television, five afternoons a week, which had acquired a news as well as an entertainment value because he managed to snare, at least one time out of five, some famous but elusive person.

What staggered me was not that Kay had married for a third time. In a way that was

7

more or less inevitable. Kay without an attentive escort or an adequate host for her parties was unthinkable. What was startling was that she had married an actor, a man outside her orbit.

Kay was my half-sister, ten years my senior and, at thirty-three, at the peak of her beauty. She was tall and full-breasted and dressed magnificently. She had dark blue eyes, a small straight nose, and blond hair, which in the last few years had been discreetly brightened. It was not her money alone that had made Kay a spectacular figure; it was a certain flamboyant quality plus the wild exploits that kept her in the news. She provided unfailing grist for the unappetizing mill of the so-called movie magazines, which in the guise of news retailed scabrous accounts of people in the public eye, with little or no concern for their truth. They followed her like baying hounds. Along with Elizabeth Taylor and Mrs. Onassis, Kay Spaulding held the unenviable place as a woman who never managed to escape the spotlight.

There was a kind of recklessness in her blood. The newspaper had grasped the opportunity afforded by her third marriage to go into details on its two disastrous predecessors and relate some of her more preposterous exploits. They even produced, on page five, an old picture of her emerging from a police station where she had landed after one of her maddest exploits. That was the time she made a crazy bet with a party of half-lit friends in a bar that she would confront, single-handed, a gunman who was holed up in a building from which he was shooting at the passers-by.

She had marched in alone, ignoring the frantic attempts of the police to stop her, and later emerged from the building with the gunman. He was only sixteen years old and he had been sniffing cocaine. She had talked him around and, by golly, she had his rifle in one hand and the boy by the other. It was not until the next day, when she had sobered up, that she got the jitters, thinking of what she had done and the chance she had taken.

She had always been known as Kay Spaulding, which was her mother's idea. As the last of the Spaulding copper family she wanted the name to live on in her daughter. So though she was willing to become Mrs. Harry Pelham, her daughter Kathryn was, at her insistence, always known as Kay Spaulding, even after she embarked on her marriages and was, in turn, Mrs. Brookfield and Mrs. Wentworth.

My father was an easy-going, sweet-tempered man and if he minded the fact that his daughter never bore his name he accepted it without argument. He disliked quarrels and always managed to slide away from them. Why his first wife ever married him I can't imagine unless it was for his good looks and his happy nature. With no disparagement of my father I suspect that it was she who made the decision. He was never impressed by her money and when he did not submit to her dominance he evaded it without dissension. Nevertheless, by her own testimony, it was, from her standpoint at least, a happy marriage. She recorded this in her own inimitable way in her will:

"My husband, Harry Pelham, has always made me a happy woman, devoted and attentive in every way, but, unless I miss my guess, some other woman will marry him if I die first. As I have no intention of letting my successor enjoy my money, and my husband has graciously signed a statement, waiving his legal rights to any share of my property, I am leaving my entire estate to my daughter Kathryn Pelham, known as Kay Spaulding."

In some ways she must have been a lot like Kay.

Five years after her death, and largely because Kay was already becoming unmanageable, my father married his secretary, who came to him without a cent and with no desire to dominate, which was just as well for she never stood a chance with Kay.

I was born ten years after Kay and christened Martha, a dreary name representing dreary virtues. Compared with Kay, I was a brown mouse. When my father died he left his entire estate to me, as a matter of justice, but as this brought in an income of something just over a hundred dollars a month it didn't matter much. Anyhow, I was never required to make do with it. From the time that she came into her own money Kay provided me with a home and she continued to do so through two tumultuous marriages. She also supplied me with clothes and with a winter at a Boston art school, where she would have continued to pay my tuition and living expenses if I had not voluntarily abandoned the idea.

Through talking with experienced would-be artists I knew there was no disillusionment as bitter as discovering in your middle years that you can't make the grade because you lack not the will but the natural endowment. By then you're so accustomed to living the life of the creative artist that it is painful to give it up. So I decided to get out intact. At least I wasn't alone. I wonder if anyone has ever counted the number of would-be opera singers and ballet dancers and concert musicians and playwrights and poets who fall by the wayside because they lack that extra something.

After this experiment Kay provided me with occasional holidays away from her house in the Turtle Bay section of Manhattan. It was while I was on one of these that I saw the announcement of her third marriage. As it was only two weeks since I had left New York and she had not even met Alan Lambert then, I was staggered. A few days later, I got her letter, exultant, glowing. Apparently after stormy upheavals with his two predecessors, she had at last found happiness, a sunny and peaceful haven after the rough voyage of her life.

"My stunning husband," she wrote. "You'll adore him, Martha. You can't help it. Just wait until you see him! We aren't going on a honeymoon because Alan is up to his chin in work, finding new and exciting people to interview. You'd be surprised at the amount of work that goes into these programs. So he has moved into the Turtle Bay house and you'll be seeing him as soon as you get back. Naturally you'll stay on here. You're not in the way, you know. Really you're not. I hardly know you are around."

That Kay meant it I was sure. She liked playing Lady Bountiful to a sufficiently grateful object, and, in many ways, she was genuinely fond of me, in spite of the ten years difference in our ages and the fact that we were only half-sisters, a relationship that is not supposed to provide much of a bond. But I was one of Kay's few friends. Like most truly beautiful women there were not many people who would be friends with her. Women were inclined to be jealous and men fell in love with her, so in a small way I filled a need.

But this time my return to the Turtle Bay house was going to be different. Even though, as she assured me, she hardly knew that I was around, I would feel like an interloper, making a third with a honeymoon couple who had been married only a few weeks.

Mansfield, who had been butler for Kay's mother and now creaked as he walked but still had the authentic aura of the stately English butler — Kay's mother had lured him away from some impoverished royalty, I believe — beamed at me when he opened the door.

"Nice to have you back, Miss Pelham. I'll have your luggage sent up in five minutes.

Mrs. Lambert wanted to see you as soon as you arrived."

Mrs. Lambert. For a moment I was taken aback. Kay was always referred to by the servants as Madam. The change must be due to the new man who apparently was not going to be known as "Kay Spaulding's husband." For once she seemed to have met her match.

I found her in the little room at the back of the house, which looked out on a miniature garden, and where she wrote her letters, paid her bills, and planned her engagements. Already marriage — this marriage — had made a difference. Usually she wore diaphanous negligées but this morning she had on a tailored housecoat. True, it was a magnificent affair of coral velvet but it zipped to the throat and had long sleeves. She looked more beautiful than I had ever seen her. Whoever said that happiness is the secret of beauty was right. She was glowing and radiant.

She laughed as she saw my expression and came to plant a kiss somewhere in the air near my left cheek. "No more alluring negligées." Her voice had a new warmth that betrayed her happiness. "Alan gets sick and tired of women throwing out lures. You have no idea! I can't wait to have you meet my stunning husband."

"It must have been awfully sudden." I let her push me into a chair.

"My dear, the *coup de foudre!* It really happens. Sam Helman had one of his clients on television and when he discovered I'd never been to a live TV show he took me along, just for fun, you know. And Alan was there and I met him. Next day I telephoned and asked him to lunch." She laughed exultantly. "I'd never done such a thing in my life before and if it hadn't been that I'd made an impression, he would have turned me down cold, because it happens to him all the time. And from then on —"

"But I've only been gone four weeks!"

"Well, we were married in two! He's enchanting. But in some ways he is rather childishly pigheaded. He insists on paying his equal share of running this big house though it costs him much more than when he was alone. But he won't listen to me about it, though I've said over and over that it is absurd. He told me the role of kept man is not for him."

I couldn't understand it. Kay had submitted to having no honeymoon because her bridegroom was too occupied with his own concerns. She had submerged the identity of Kay Spaulding in that of Mrs. Alan

15

Lambert. For the first time in her life she was submitting to the will of someone else and obviously loving it.

It was with the vague picture of a Robert Taylor type of man that I went down to dinner that night. When Kay introduced Alan I was so surprised that I caught myself gaping at him and was aware of it only when I saw his smile, which held understanding and amusement and warm friendliness.

Kay's stunning husband was an ugly man of forty, big and rangy, with rugged features, a rough thatch of hair he could never control, and an assured ease of movement that managed to look awkward. Later I could understand the baffled producer of Alan's program. "I can't figure out the public," he admitted. "I thought women wanted to look at a man as handsome as Frank McGee and instead they are wild about Alan's ugly mug."

That first evening we sat late over dinner and the talk was light and gay, unlike any I remembered from Kay's former marriages. Alan was no "yes" man though he was obviously in love with Kay who, as obviously, adored him. Not once was there the faintest glimmer of her awesome temper, not once did she contradict him. In fact, she showed a quality that was almost docility in making tentative plans for some evening parties, as Alan had a daytime program.

"So few of my friends have met you, darling, and I thought a series of small, intimate dinners —"

"Of course. But how long is this display to go on?"

"Do you mind very much?" She sounded anxious, she who always stated her plans and expected them to be abided by.

"Not if your heart is set on it, pet, but space them out if you can. I'm a hardworking guy, you know, and I've never gone in much for night life."

"I suppose you still stick to your old cowboy ways of going to bed when it gets dark," she jeered at him.

He grinned amiably. "Old habits are hard to break."

"Like your dear friend Scott Jameson."

That was the first time I ever heard the name of Scott Jameson.

"What have you got against Scott? You've never laid eyes on the man. He's a good guy; the best friend I ever had."

"He's your evil genius, if you ask me. The way you defer to him! It's Scott this and Scott that. Everything is fine unless Scott wants to do something and then you're at his beck and call. If I ever get a chance I'll let him know what I think of him."

Alan laughed. "Then I'll take good care to see that doesn't happen, pet."

"Well, what is it about him?" she wailed.

"Darned if I know." Alan sounded perplexed. "Thing is that I've been a kind of older brother to him most of my life and he relies on me, Kay."

"I still say he's your evil genius and some day you'll realize it. I only hope," she added darkly, "it won't be too late."

What a husband for Kay! I tried to compare him with those sleek, well-groomed, smooth-talking, subservient men who had been his predecessors and gave up. There was no understanding it. And then, before the evening ended, something catastrophic had happened. Without knowing why or how it had happened I had fallen head over heels in love with Alan Lambert.

Two

In the painful month that followed I managed to stay out of Alan's way as far as possible, pretending to have dates when I actually spent evening after evening at the movies. In a rerun theater far uptown there was an old Alan Lambert western and for one besotted week I spent the evenings watching his ugly face.

Every afternoon from two to three I, who had never in my life watched daytime television, watched his talk show, and wondered, as practically all his competition in the field wondered, how on earth he managed to attract such interesting and elusive people to his program and draw them out like a father confessor.

It had required all Alan's tact to convince Kay that it would be better for her not to be one of the audience that attended his show. The producer felt that her presence would cast a damper on his women admirers and, "Believe me, pet, when they stop clamoring for autographs and watching my show, your husband is going to lose his rating and then he'll be out of a job."

"As long as it's only part of your job," she laughed.

"You mean as long as I don't slip my leash?"

"I didn't mean that," she said quickly.

Of course I could not entirely avoid Alan and, though I tried hard, now and then I was afraid that he had guessed how I felt about him. After all, with so many women making a cult of him, he must have been fairly familiar with the symptoms, but his attitude never varied. He was always kind, always understanding. He treated me as though I were a younger sister, making a little gentle fun of me, while Kay looked on approvingly. I discovered, in horror and disgust at this revelation of my true nature, that I was beginning to dislike her.

Though Alan usually said little about his job, the subject of an evening program on prime time came up frequently. With her immense holdings in copper Kay wanted to get the Spaulding Copper Company to back his show and she was deeply hurt when Alan shied away from the idea.

"I can't see why you should object, darling," she said in bewilderment. "I'm not trying to run you."

He grinned. "You couldn't, Kay. I acknowledge only one boss."

"Who's that?" Her tone was sharp.

"The clock. Everyone and everything in television is governed by the clock."

Kay was not to be diverted from her idea. "With my thirty percent of the stock I'm the biggest single stockholder and I carry a lot of weight."

"I know you do, pet."

"I like doing things for you, Alan." There was reproach in her voice. Her eyes filled with tears.

"You like to buy me things."

As usual Kay's quick temper flared at the first hint of opposition. "You knew I was a rich woman when you married me but I don't recall that stopping you."

"Also a beautiful woman." His voice was a resonant baritone, the kind that is most effective in broadcasting, but by the compression of his mouth I knew how much restraint he was putting on himself and I slipped out of the room as unobtrusively as I could. I recognized the symptoms. Kay was working herself up to one of her screaming rages, which were always horrifying to watch, no matter how often one saw them.

With the experience of ten years I knew that, once the pattern of her tantrums began, this marriage, like the other two, was headed for the rocks. And yet she was deeply in love with him and happier than she had ever been in her life. In some ways, Kay was a stupid woman.

It was Alan, with one of his careless, good-humored gestures, who arranged the job at the broadcasting company for me. One of the happiest days of my life was when I drew money from my savings account and put down a month's rent in advance on an apartment that was to be my very own, my symbol of independence.

The night before I moved, I told Kay what I planned to do. As I had foreseen, she was surprised and hurt. There was plenty of room in her house, she pointed out, and I was in nobody's way. And why on earth get a job? People would think she was tight-fisted or something and I was putting her in an intolerable and embarrassing position. I was thinking only of my own wishes and not caring about hers. I was self-centered and selfish, as I had been all my life, though there was nothing she had ever begrudged me.

I had never been able to withstand Kay so it was Alan who managed the business of persuading her to accept my decision, and it took a lot of tact, of which he had an inexhaustible amount — he needed it on his job — to manage it.

"It's tough on the kid, pet," I heard him explain to her, "always living in your shadow. The ugly duckling. It will be good for her to get out and make some friends on her own."

"But Martha has never made many friends on her own," Kay pointed out.

"She is overshadowed. No one looks at her when you are around. Give her a chance and see what happens. She'll probably blossom out and surprise you. Anyhow, it is time I contrived to be alone with my wife."

She laughed low in contentment and said no more in opposition to my leaving.

A few days later I began my job as receptionist at the broadcasting station in a big, square, ugly building with an unexpectedly plain and unadorned waiting room, where chairs were arranged in groups of two, separated by screens, for brief interviews. In one corner there was a television set on which the day's programs appeared, blessedly without sound, and I realized that broadcasting is a twenty-four hour operation and someone even at that early hour was giving information on food values, to judge by the prices and labels that flashed across the screen.

Over the desk with its switchboard there was a huge clock and on the desk stood a vase of long-stemmed red roses and a neat plaque reading: *Miss Martha Pelham*, both gifts from Alan.

The woman who was sitting at the switchboard turned to give me a quick, appraising look and then she smiled. "You must be Martha Pelham, the new receptionist. I am Hope Bancroft and I have been assigned the job of showing you the ropes on your first day."

"I hope it isn't interfering with your own work."

She smiled with a flash of white teeth. She was a small vivid woman with black hair and eyes, a brunette with skin the color of dark honey and quick, darting movements. She must have been in her early thirties but she looked younger.

"My job is everyone's job. I'm a general fixer-upper around here, as you'll find out. I've even been called in to replace the make-up man when he had flu, and once I did a bit part in that soap opera we've been running since the beginning of time, *Angela's Affairs*. After that, being receptionist is child's play."

Actually, as I learned later, she was the assistant manager of the station and probably the most valuable person there, holding all the complex strings in her small, competent hands and keeping them unentangled.

She glanced automatically at the big clock and said, "I'm glad you came early. It will give me a chance to show you around before people start coming in. Primarily your job is to act as a kind of traffic manager, routing people to the proper departments and weeding out the hopeless applicants and the nuisances, which requires tact and firmness, chiefly firmness. You'll soon learn to spot them at a glance."

She took me on a swift tour of the building. My first impression was one of surprise at the general bleakness except on the top floor where the executives had their offices, which were equipped with the carpeting, draperies, paintings, and all the air of opulence that most businesses find it necessary to provide as background for their executives. The rest of the building was stripped and bare and functional, except for the living room set in which *Angela's Affairs* was performed.

There was a big bleak room where commercials were done against changing backdrops and the room with its raised tiers of seats for live audiences with the familiar blue backdrop bearing Alan Lambert's name, where his shows were done.

What struck me most was the incredible number of people who seemed to be necessary for the production of the simplest program: the cameramen, the technicians, the director and producer, and all the others whose names usually appear in small print at the end of a show, and a horde who remain nameless. I didn't understand half their functions then and I still don't understand them all. There were several rehearsal rooms, one of which was used for Hall Canfield's brilliant set of award-winning plays.

That first day was bewildering and exciting. To be announcing famous names over the telephone had me in such a dither that I stuttered, and the sight of famous faces coming and going distracted my attention from my job.

A young man rushed in, took a harried look at the clock, and darted past. Hope called him back.

"Hi, Johnny, meet a fellow sufferer. This is Martha Pelham. John Carr, who plays Angela's next-door neighbor. For heaven's sake, Johnny, wait until the make-up man gets a load of your pan. He's never going to get that open boyish look on your battered mug. What did you do last night — paint the town red?"

"The baby is teething and I was up half the night with her because Florence has flu and needs rest at night if she's to cope during the day. And twelve sides of lines to learn for this morning."

"You should have stuck to the pill," Hope commented. After he had rushed out she said, "Any poor devil who works in a daily soap opera is the modern galley slave. You rehearse all morning, do the show in the afternoon, and spend the evening learning tomorrow's lines. It's a dog's life."

"Then why do they do it?"

She gave me an odd look. "Bread and butter, dearie. With your background you wouldn't know about that."

Hope got someone to replace me at noon and took me out to lunch at a big noisy restaurant frequented in equal parts by television personnel and those who had come to look at them. While we ordered she pointed out people with familiar faces and grinned at my expression. "You feel you're right at the heart of the action, don't you?"

I nodded, aware that I was flushing.

She looked up and waved a casual hand and Alan pulled out a chair between us, ordered a vodka martini, nodded to half a dozen acquaintances, and smiled at me.

"Hope looking after you all right?"

"She's been awfully kind."

"She's a little mother to us all. I thought it might be nice to have lunch together on your first day. Working out all right?"

"I hope so. I know how to handle the switchboard and who most of the people are. The only thing is —"

"She can't say no," Hope told him and Alan laughed.

"Stick to it and you'll become as tough as Hope."

"Oh, Alan. I haven't thanked you for the roses and the name plate."

"Very impressive, isn't it? Makes you look official."

"You're so good to me."

"I've only got one kid sister." He flicked a casual finger against my cheek. To my horror a wave of color crept up over my face and down my throat. Alan was speaking to someone who had paused beside the table and did not notice, but Hope, who missed very little, subjected me to a long, curious scrutiny.

Everything was different at the station when Alan came in. A little group of women standing outside the building surged forward, speaking to him, holding out autograph albums, trying to shake hands. He gave me a rueful grin and turned to his fans.

"Is it like this every day?" I asked Hope.

"Every single day. They're his bread and butter, you know."

"Yes, that's what he told his wife. My sister, Kay."

"Is she jealous of her competition?"

I laughed at that. "Jealous? You've never seen her. With her beauty she has never needed to be jealous of any woman. If she ever — well, the only person she is jealous of is Alan's friend Scott Jameson. She thinks he is a bad influence."

"You know," Hope said unexpectedly, "I wouldn't be surprised if she is right about that."

"Do you know him?"

"I've seen him around with Alan."

"What is he like?"

"He's a gambler with a gambler's unshakable faith in his luck. And he is never satisfied. He's always sure there is a bigger card game going on somewhere else. If he broke the bank at Monte Carlo, he'd go looking for a bigger bank."

Alan came in, big and smiling and warm, followed by his admiring horde whom an attendant steered off to their seats.

A cameraman looked out to say, "Hi, Alan, did you know Harry's kid is in the hospital with a broken leg?"

"Oh, that's too bad. Send some flowers to his wife to cheer her up, will you?"

"Alan," a man came hurrying into the

29

waiting room and glanced, that compulsive look, at the clock overhead. "Your man Clifton is here and having jitters. He wants out."

Alan glanced at the television screen, saw that the cooking lesson was still going on. "I've got another twenty minutes to calm him down." He shook his head at me. "You never know how they will behave. Sometimes they are naturals and completely unselfconscious. Sometimes they take one look at the microphone and freeze. You'd think they expected it to electrocute them. You need to be on your toes every minute because there are no retakes and there is always the chance of someone saying something that is beyond the bounds. It's a dog's life." He went unhurriedly out of the waiting room to soothe his frenzied guest.

When Alan's program came on I found it hard to concentrate on the switchboard. His warmth and friendliness came through and it was apparent, even so, that he had not been successful in calming down his special guest of the day. Watching him now, his hostile eyes fixed on Alan's face, his words seemed to come sparsely and reluctantly so that Alan was forced to carry most of the weight of the interview. You've seen a similar situation. One man has to ask a question

30

that is about ten sentences long to elicit a simple yes or no. Aggravating, to say the least.

Hope startled me into awareness of my absorption by taking over the switchboard and making soothing comments into it. "Okay, Martha," she said when I apologized. "The first day is bound to be distracting, especially in a place like this, and then — Alan has that effect on all women, of course."

Alan and his program were followed by an advertisement and then I saw the living room and the girl who played Angela was sitting at a small desk, smiling at her client for the day. In case you have missed this perennial, Angela runs an advice to the lovelorn column and her correspondents are always coming to her home with their personal difficulties, so she is constantly involved in emotional situations. Now and then, to vary the picture, she is threatened by an angry husband who does not like the advice she has given his wife.

The door at the back opened and Clifton came out, looking pale and exhausted. He went through the room without a glance to either side, and the outside door banged.

Hope laughed. "It takes some of them that way. Here's a man famous all over the world for his courage and his physical endurance under incredible strain, and he quails at looking at a microphone."

Unconsciously I was waiting for Alan to come out, but it was late in the afternoon before he finally emerged. I had put through a number of calls for him. As he passed me he said to Hope, "I've got all next week's people lined up."

"Even Meredith?"

"Even Meredith."

"Alan, you're a living wonder. How did you do it?"

"I just tried to point out what publicity in the right places could do and that hooked him." He turned to me. "All right, Martha?" He glanced automatically at the clock — an obsessive gesture with television people — and went out at his usual unhurried pace. Going home to Kay. I thrust that thought firmly out of my mind.

Three

As a result of my move out of Kay's imme-
diate orbit I was no longer included in her invitations or in her social life. So it happened
that for the next few weeks I saw her only
twice and never saw Alan again except at the
station, where his appearance was always the
occasion for mounting excitement among the
people waiting to see his show, and where his
warm kindliness made him popular with the
station people from the technicians to the executives. Always assured, always unhurried,
the tyranny of the clock did not appear to op-
press him.

It was at the end of my first week in my
little apartment that Kay came to see me
and inspect the place in which I had chosen
to live.

I was coming in with a big brown paper
bag of groceries when her long sleek town
car drew up to the curb and the chauffeur
opened the door for her. She got out, staring
in dismay at the rundown old building.

"But, Martha," she exclaimed as I came
up to her. "But, Martha — why?"

33

Her expression was one of bewildered horror when I led the way down the uncarpeted basement stairs and unlocked the door. Then it changed when she saw my bright, gay little living room. Knowing that I was going to have a regular salary I had removed practically all my savings for the first month's rent on that little basement apartment and had furnished it according to my own ideas.

To compensate for sunless rooms I had flooded the place with color. I had waxed and polished the floor and bought small, bright scatter rugs. The living room had gold draperies that shut out the bars on the windows (a safety precaution), as well as the noise of the street, and gave the illusion of sunlight.

There was one big luscious armchair in the same gold and a lounge chair and couch covered in a soft green. I had brought from Kay's house a little carved table, an antique that had belonged to my mother, and the paintings I had acquired out of my small income, whose greens and yellows picked up the colors in upholstery and rugs. I had filled a small bookcase with favorite books and bought two really good lamps. Alan had given me a television set, provided a bottle of champagne, and kissed me for luck.

There was also a tiny bedroom, a minute bath, and a kitchen big enough to hold a table and two chairs. I had covered the kitchen pipes and got a red and white checked tablecloth. With a bright red geranium on the kitchen table and a vase of daffodils in the living room the place was colorful and gay.

Kay stood looking around her, the heavy scent she always wore dimming the delicate sweetness of the daffodils. "Why, it's charming! How clever of you, Martha."

I was touched to see that, as a house gift, she had brought me one of her most cherished possessions, a small and endearing Renoir etching, which we hung in the living room, where the little lady in her demure bonnet looked out at us benignly, bestowing on the room a quality of distinction.

Kay exclaimed over everything in the apartment. "But what on earth can you do with your clothes when you have only that one small closet?"

"It holds my whole wardrobe without any trouble," I told her dryly. "And as for storage space, I have my fur coat in cold storage and you'd never guess where I've put the winter blankets."

That day Kay was in her most endearingly childlike mood and she hunted for the blankets, laughing and making wild guesses. At length she climbed on the kitchen ladder, which I had painted bright red, lost her balance, and grasped at the wall to steady herself, finding, just as I had done in similar circumstances, the deep recessed space behind the standing pipes where I had stored blankets and suitcases.

"What a wonderful place to hide your secrets!"

"I haven't any," I told her, not quite truthfully.

As she was leaving she asked, "Martha, has Scott Jameson ever come to the station to see Alan?"

"Not so far as I know. At least no one of that name has asked for him on the telephone or at the desk."

"Well, I'm telling you in confidence that I have hired a detective to find out the truth about that man. It's the only way I'll ever be able to convince Alan that he is bad medicine."

"But if there is nothing to expose?"

"There will be," Kay said in a tone of such conviction that I was taken aback.

"You know," I said with a twinge of uneasiness, "if he is really — that is, if something about him is wrong, it might be risky for you to attempt to expose him."

Kay laughed. "I've been taking risks all my life. They add salt to the feast. And I'm not afraid." She opened her handbag to make a note of my telephone number, writing with a gold pencil in a small notebook with her initials in gold. As she pulled it out, a thick wad of twenty-dollar bills in a gold clip slipped to the floor.

"Heavens," I exclaimed, "you shouldn't carry that amount of cash around with you. It's just asking for trouble."

She shrugged. "What's the use of having the stuff if it isn't available?"

"Well, if you must — wait!" I rummaged in the drawer of the living room table and pulled out a small ammonia spray I had bought when I realized I'd be walking home at night from the station. You know the thing; it looks like a tiny fire extinguisher. The idea is, when a mugger demands your billfold, to pull out the ammonia spray and let him have it in the face.

Kay could often be stubborn but this time she was amused. She accepted it as a gadget to play with, though I warned her to be careful.

"Cautious Martha!" She patted my cheek with a gloved hand, blew me a kiss, and went out on a wave of perfume. I heard her heels tap on the basement stairs, heard her cross the sidewalk, heard the slam of her car door.

It was nearly a month before I saw her again. She called me at the station and asked me to meet her for cocktails at the Plaza when I had finished work. As usual, people noticed her when she came in. She was the most perfectly groomed woman I ever knew. She seemed preoccupied, I thought, and asked only perfunctorily about my job, which I answered as perfunctorily, as she obviously wasn't interested.

In some ways she seemed unlike herself. It was in an effort to find some subject of conversation that would interest her that I asked whether she had ever learned anything about Scott Jameson from her detective.

She began to laugh. "Wait until I tell Alan what I know about his dear friend, and I'm just holding out for the right moment. He's going to get the shock of his life. I'm counting on you to stand by when the time comes. In a lot of ways, Martha, you really are a darling. Alan thinks so too." She gave me an odd sort of smile. "You think a lot of Alan, don't you?"

My smile was as bland as hers. "Of course I do."

Her own smile deepened. "Wait until you meet his friend Scott."

And next day, because I had fallen into

the habit of confiding small matters to Hope — everyone did — I told her, like the utter fool I was, what Kay had said.

Hope was silent for a time, automatically straightening some cards she had been examining, tapping them on the desk, riffling through them, straightening them again. At last she looked at me, her face troubled.

"I don't suppose — is there any chance that Scott could find out what your sister is up to?"

"She's not a cautious woman."

"Then I'm going to see him myself and persuade him to get out of town, even if I have to raise the money myself."

"Why?"

"Because he never tolerates having anyone interfere with his plans. He's been making blatant use of Alan for years and, if anyone threatened that, he'd — he'd — make Alan suffer for it, though you couldn't convince Alan that Scott isn't as loyal to him as he is to Scott. There's a ruthless strain in him, though he usually covers it very well."

"Aren't you afraid to tackle a man like that?"

"I'd rather tangle with a rattlesnake," Hope admitted, "but this station is husband and child to me and I'm not going to let Scott Jameson jeopardize it."

During those first weeks in the station I had learned to know my way around: to become accustomed to seeing celebrities go in and out of the place; to learn, as Hope had taught me, not to feel sorry for the people I had to send away.

"You have to be tough," she told me over and over.

I was still taken aback by the enormous difference between famous people as I had imagined them and as they were in real life. I learned this over again every week with Alan's great names whom he had snared out of seclusion and from behind the walls of inviolate privacy they had built around themselves. He didn't get Howard Hughes, of course, but he got almost equally elusive people, while men in competitive jobs gnawed their nails and wondered how he did it.

But I was still surprised the day I met Hall Canfield. His plays were outrageously funny and he was just a quiet, unobtrusive, nondescript man with vague eyes. He carried a battered briefcase and he dressed as though he were working in Hollywood rather than on Manhattan, in slacks and a turtleneck sweater. His award-winning plays were acutely observed pictures of human foibles but they were gay without malice and without any taint of sentimentality. Hall Canfield gave the impression of walking blindly through the world, unaware of his surroundings.

As a rule he went past the reception desk with only a brief nod. What drew his attention was nothing about me personally; it was chancing to overhear a bit of dialogue. As a man constantly in search of ideas he paused in his swift pace and then, caught by what the girl was saying, he hovered, obviously eavesdropping and enjoying himself hugely.

The girl who gave her name as Gloria Hastings was as phony as her name. Her eyes were made up with green paste and she wore artificial lashes about an inch long, purple lipstick that completely distorted the natural shape of her mouth and which, to say the least, was striking. She wore a platinum wig that was about a foot high and a skirt that was about a foot long. She was preposterous, incredible, and she could not have been a day over sixteen.

What she wanted was to meet "a man with influence," and she batted those preposterous eyelashes at me knowingly. It was her ambition to become a television star of the first magnitude, someone who would put

Lucy in the shade. For this she was blithely prepared to make the supreme sacrifice on the casting director's couch. After about two minutes' talk with her it was apparent that she had only the vaguest idea of what was involved, though how she had managed to live for sixteen years in such a state of un-sullied ignorance about the more basic facts of life was incomprehensible to me.

Because the poor kid was obviously the kind to be victimized, it wasn't fair to send her out, unwarned and unarmed. I ex-plained to her as well as I could that she would have to have some special talent to sell, since the one she was prepared to use was a drug on the market. And I urged her to finish high school; then perhaps she could get a job like mine in a broadcasting station and learn the ropes and meet all the won-derful people.

I'll say for Gloria that she did not resent my advice. She accepted it with grateful thanks. In spite of her horrific appearance she was a humble little thing. She wasn't even angry when I said what a pity it was she had been ill-advised about make-up, con-cealing her pretty face. And really, if you looked hard enough, she was a pretty child.

It was the day after this encounter that Hall Canfield stopped to chat with me, recalling my interview with the schoolgirl and asking about other experiences. He was, I realized, looking for material so I wasn't misled into taking his interest personally. We drifted into a kind of partnership. I got to saving especially funny stories for him and he took me to lunch a couple of times and proved to be an entertaining companion who talked about everything except himself and his job.

The first real date with Hall was to be dinner at Sardi's, but when the time came and just as Hall arrived to collect me, the skies opened and there was a regular cloudburst. As there was no chance of it letting up I suggested cooking dinner myself.

For this occasion he had taken the trouble to dress in a dark suit and white shirt and he looked unexpectedly formal. He surveyed my bright little apartment and then turned to me. "You are full of surprises, aren't you, Martha? When you said it was a basement apartment I thought you had gone bohemian but I see you are —"

"Just one of the Marthas of this world," I admitted in resignation.

"No, you're miscast as Martha."

"You're wrong; it's tailored to fit."

"The devil it is! The name is all wrong for you."

"Well, my mother called me Mattie but no one else ever has."

"I'm going to. That's a lot better. But don't try to get any compliments out of me. I like this place. It suits you. Except for the basement, of course. You belong out in the sunlight and the fresh air."

"Well, I picked a basement apartment because it's cheap."

He raised his eyebrows in surprise but made no comment. While I got dinner, he hovered in the kitchen doorway, getting in the way because the room was so small. He seemed to be very much at home. I took chops from the freezing compartment, put potatoes in the oven to bake, tossed a salad and put it in the refrigerator to chill, made hot biscuits, and proudly produced the bottle of champagne Alan had given me for the housewarming I had never held.

We talked light-heartedly over dinner, gossiping about the people at the station and the contrast between their real lives and their public personalities.

"But there's Hope," I reminded him. "She's always the same. Always dependable."

"Bedrock," he agreed. "I knew her husband slightly. You probably heard that he was one of the foremost psychoanalysts of his time, a whole lot older than Hope, of

44

course. Then I discovered that one of his former patients was an old college friend of mine. He told me once that Dr. Bancroft had experimented with taking down his interviews on tapes so that his attention could be free to notice the fleeting changes of inflection and pace in his patients, and not bother with the laborious business of writing it all down.

"After Bancroft's death I heard that he had been wiped out on the market and I offered Hope a nice piece of change to let me have the tapes for material. I swore I would change names and alter the stuff so no one could recognize it but she was outraged. She said she had destroyed everything without listening. It was the least she could do for her husband's memory and his reputation. And I happen to know that she was flat broke at the time because that is when she got a job at the station."

The only flaw in a pleasant evening came when Hall's eyes fell on the framed photograph Alan had given me the week before, one that had been taken for publicity purposes. Across it he had scrawled, "For Martha with love from Alan."

"Boy friend?"

"Of course not! He's my brother-in-law. At least, he is my half-sister's husband."

He looked at me, dumbfounded. "Kay Spaulding! Your sister? I can't believe it."

"No one does."

"I didn't mean what you thought I meant." He smiled at me, his smile rueful. I was taken by surprise. "You are so completely unlike your half-sister."

"I know. She's a beautiful woman, isn't she?"

He looked at me critically. "You're not so hard on the eyes yourself."

"Oh, don't be silly! I've been the ugly duckling all my life. Old sobersides. Old reliable. I've heard all the words."

"Not all of them. You aren't the serious type you think you are, Mattie. There's laughter bubbling up in you all the time, like that champagne, and just waiting to get out. Why don't you give it a chance instead of bottling it up? Or have you been overshadowed?"

Overshadowed. That had been Alan's word.

"It isn't Kay's fault," I said defensively, "that compared with her —"

"Only a blind fool would compare you with your sister," he said and seemed to regret his abruptness. "I grant that she's a beauty but you're okay yourself. The real difference lies a lot deeper."

"How can you possibly know if you just judge by the gossip? If you knew her —"

"Oh, I did know her a long time ago. After her first marriage, I think. Anyhow it was one of the times when she was free of emotional encumbrances. I was one of the men who fell in love with her beauty, but I was never a candidate for the matrimonial sweepstakes. In some ways, I have a strong sense of self-preservation."

"I suppose the truth is that she wouldn't have had you," I snapped.

He grinned at me. "Well, not for very long, that's a cinch. I'm no lap dog. The role of attentive escort and dutiful husband for a spoiled heiress does not attract me. Anyhow, I can earn my own living."

"And so does Alan! He's never taken a cent from her. He pays his own way. He won't even let the Spaulding Copper Company sponsor a prime-time show for him."

"Whoa!" Hall tipped back my chin, smiled at me, and then, unexpectedly, bent down and kissed me lightly on the lips. "You're a loyal supporter of Lambert's, aren't you?"

Again, mercilessly, that betraying color flamed in my cheeks. One of his eyebrows rose speculatively but he made no comment. He shifted the conversation lightly to something else.

47

On the whole, once the subject of Kay was shelved, it was a most successful evening. We talked a lot and laughed a lot, and finally, perhaps as a result of the champagne, we kicked back the rugs and danced to music on the radio. He wasn't a very good dancer but then neither was I so it was all great fun.

He was right about one thing. I hadn't realized how much laughter was bottled up in me or how much fun it could be to talk spontaneously about anything that came into my head to someone who was really interested. Once I broke off in the middle of an absurd story to scowl at him suspiciously.

"If you are just drawing me out to get material —"

"It's a safe bet that Kay Spaulding never suspects a man of having ulterior motives when he wants to talk to her."

"She is Mrs. Alan Lambert now, and never forget it. And leave her out of this. You don't understand her."

"I don't pretend to understand her, Mattie. What I do know is that she is the kind of woman to whom things happen."

"At least that's interesting! Nothing ever happens to me."

"For which you ought to thank God," he said more soberly than I would have expected.

Four

The next day Kay disappeared but I did not know that then. In the morning Hall stopped to talk and remind me that he owed me a dinner but not at Sardi's; some place where we could dance. So I was left with the pleasant feeling that he too had enjoyed the evening.

The actress who played Angela slipped on the floor of the waiting room, which had just been waxed, and sprained her wrist, but like the trouper she was, she went through the rehearsal and her performance. Then, to the consternation of her producer, she fainted. He was afraid she would not be able to learn her lines for the next day and he attempted to use bolstering up tactics that would have made me want to throttle him.

Alan's special guest was Vaughan Collins, an almost legendary figure, one of the financial wizards of the world, who contrived most of the time to remain behind the scenes.

The only unusual thing about that day from my standpoint was the realization when I got home from work that Kay had been in the apartment. In fact, the scent of her perfume was so strong that at first I believed she was still there and called out, but the place was empty and she had left no message. On the floor near the door I found one of her handkerchiefs, with a "K" embroidered in exquisite tiny stitches, one of those made for her at some nunnery in Italy, and saturated with her familiar perfume, which explained the scent that had attracted me when I opened the door. I wondered fleetingly how she got in and then forgot about it.

I half expected her to telephone and explain her visit as she had never returned to the apartment after her tour of inspection, and I thought if she did not call I'd get in touch with her. But I'd left last night's dishes to soak and I tackled them and straightened up the place. After supper I rinsed out some clothes and washed my hair and, what with one thing and another, I forgot about Kay's visit.

It must have been after two when the phone rang and I stumbled sleepily into the living room to answer it. But it was not Kay who was calling me, it was Alan.

"Hi there, Martha, sorry to call you so late but have you seen Kay?"

"No," I said in surprise. "She isn't here. Why? Is anything wrong?"

"Probably not." But he sounded dissatisfied. "She was going to meet some friends and catch up on old times or something like that but she seems to have been delayed. She's never stayed out this way without telling me in advance. In fact, since we've been married she hasn't spent an evening without me. She left a message with Mansfield but he garbled it as he always does. People named Knight or Bright or Wright or Blight. Some damned thing. But that was early in the afternoon and no word since, so I got worried. Do you happen to know who these friends are?"

"No, I don't know half her friends even by name, and she didn't tell me anything about her plans. However, she was here today, Alan."

"She was!"

"As soon as I came in I noticed that scent she always wears and I found one of her handkerchiefs, but she didn't leave a message so I don't know why she came. I was half expecting that she would call to explain."

"She came during the day while you were out?"

"That's what I said."

51

"And no message? Nothing?"

"Not a word."

"Did you give her a key?"

"No. I wondered how she'd managed to get in."

After a pause he said, "Sorry to bother you, Martha. She's probably all right and having a high old time. The only thing is that she's never done it before. Well, don't worry, kid. Good night."

For a while, after I returned to bed, I lay thinking about Kay, wondering about her visit to me, wondering why she had gone off without discussing her plans with Alan. But probably she had returned to the Turtle Bay house by now.

The next morning was like any other at the station. Poor Angela dashed in at the last minute, clutching her script in her good hand and looking most unlike the serene, all-wise young woman she would appear to be in her television performance.

Hall stopped at my desk to say that he had decided to give up writing for television after the production of his current play, and take time off before starting something else.

"But why? They're so successful and you're bound to get another award this year. Do you need rest?"

"I need ideas. That's every writer's nightmare," and he was on his way.

Hope came to sit beside the switchboard and talk for a few minutes, though she automatically watched the television screen with its mouthing actors. She never slipped up on details. But even Hope could make mistakes and bad ones.

"Did you find Scott Jameson?" I asked.

"I ran him down at one of his haunts and warned him that Kay had the lowdown on him and that he'd be wise to clear out. You know I never believed that kind of thing really worked: 'Fly; all is discovered.' But there is something Scott is afraid of. He sat staring at me, pushing his ring up and down on his finger, his eyes sort of fixed. So I pressed hard. I said Kay was really gunning for him and loaded for bear."

"Oh, Hope! I wish you hadn't said that. Suppose he makes trouble for her."

"He won't. I bought him three drinks and more or less poured him on a plane for Arizona."

"Why Arizona?"

"That's his home state, where he met Alan, you know, back in the days when Alan was stuck in those Grade B westerns."

"Do you think he'll stay there?"

She shrugged. "I can't predict what Scott is likely to do. But he'd be a fool not to stay.

Whatever Kay may have raked up won't do him any good with Alan, and he can always get a job as an extra in a western. They still shoot a lot of them out there, you know. One thing that man can do really well is ride a horse and he's the daredevil type who makes a good stunt man. Taking chances is the breath of life to him. And he won't be far by air from Las Vegas so that ought to hold him, if nothing else does."

"Was he very bitter about Kay checking up on him?"

"He didn't pour out his heart to me," Hope said dryly. "God, I have a blinding headache. I'll be glad when this day is over."

"Can't you just walk out for once?"

"With that dog-food manufacturer coming in about advertising and Alan's senator to get the red-carpet treatment and Polly Jackson to be given the axe now her thirteen-week-contract is at an end and —"

"Poor Hope! They leave all the dirty jobs to you."

"You're telling me." She waved her hand and went out of the room.

After lunch Alan made his usual impressive entrance, trailed by the women who had come to watch his show and who were herded out of the room and into their seats where they were given their instructions. He paused beside my desk. "Well, what did you think?"

"About what?"

He looked rather hurt. "Here, unaccustomed as I am, I make an impressive public speech, and in honor of old Cosgrave too! *The New York Times* prints it in full, yet my nearest and dearest don't even read it."

Cosgrave was the retiring vice-president of the station, leaving with the unanimous enthusiasm of the whole staff, but Alan, with his customary good nature, had agreed to make the farewell address at a reception and present Cosgrave with an onyx desk set, which, as no one believed the man could either read or write, would be purely for ornamental purposes. I'd seen the headlines but had not read the story and I felt ashamed.

When he saw that, Alan grinned. "Okay, kid. I was only joking." As he glanced at the clock and moved toward the door I said, "What on earth had happened to Kay?"

He turned back, the smile wiped off his face. "God only knows. She hasn't come home yet."

When I stared at him he shook his head. "I realize she is unpredictable but I am worried as hell, Martha. If I hadn't known how she would hate it I'd have called the police long before this."

"Oh, don't do that, Alan! She'd never forgive you. She'd think you were making a fool of her or of yourself."

"Well, damn it, women like Kay don't just walk off without a word. She's never done anything like this before. Are you positive she didn't leave any message for you?"

"Positive."

"Then why did she go to your apartment when you weren't there? It doesn't make sense. Unless she'd arranged to meet someone — oh, that's just ridiculous."

"Of course it is."

"Look here," he said abruptly, "I'm not going to let this thing go on another minute. I'm calling the police right now. Later you can help me clear myself with Kay if she is really angry, but I'm not going to put in another night like the last one. I don't think I slept two hours. Get me an outside wire, will you?"

I did so reluctantly, knowing Kay would hotly resent any interference with her movements, and quite probably fly into one of her screaming tantrums, but I saw by Alan's grim expression that he had made up his mind.

I heard him identify himself, say his wife was missing, and describe her: thirty-three years old, height five foot six, weight one hundred and twenty, blond, a very beautiful woman with dark blue eyes and no distinguishing marks. She would probably be carrying quite a wad of money. She usually did. No, he didn't know how she had been dressed when she left the house.

One of the technicians looked out. "Alan, Mrs. Bancroft said to tell you that your tame senator is here and getting a bit hot under the collar because you weren't on hand to greet him personally."

"Oops! On my way." Alan smiled at me. "I feel a lot better now I've done something about it." He went out with his usual assured, unhurried tread and the technician drew a breath of relief. Everything seemed to smooth out when Alan was there.

In thirty minutes his program came on and he presented the senator to his audience and then settled down to the interview. At least there was no problem of finding this quarry gun-shy. The senator had been coping with microphones and cameras for years, though he rarely gave personal interviews, so this was another of Alan's coups. It was typical of him that, however worried he might be, there was no indication of it in his manner. He seemed to be devoting all his attention to the senator.

The program ran for sixty minutes, from

two until three o'clock. It was just drawing to a close when two men came in. They were dressed in a perfectly ordinary way but everything about them was stamped "official," from the curiously erect carriage to the watchful eyes and the mouths that gave away nothing. They gave the impression of being, in a way, stripped for action.

As they came toward the desk they saw the screen, where Alan and the senator talked without sound and they paused to watch. Only when it was over did they approach the desk.

"We'd like to see Mr. Lambert."

"Do you have an appointment?"

"No, this is police business."

"Police! Kay! Is it about Kay?"

The older of the two men said, "What do you mean?"

"Mr. Lambert's wife. She's my sister and she seems to be missing and Alan reported it just an hour and a half ago to the police. He's about crazy with worry because she didn't come home all night and there was no message or anything."

"Yes, it's about Mrs. Lambert," the older man, who said his name was Saunders, told me. He introduced his silent companion as Wilkins.

"You've found her! Is she — hurt?" It's

funny how you balk at the big words when they might really apply.

"We have no official identification as yet but we believe — I'm sorry, Miss —" Saunders looked at the nameplate. "Miss Pelham. I'm afraid she is dead."

You don't take in a monstrous fact like that all at once. The mind resists it, rejects it. I called Alan's extension and asked him to come at once. "It's the police about Kay." Automatically I continued answering the switchboard calls until he came, escorting the senator. He left him at the door and came at once to the desk, looking from me to the two men as though trying to read in our faces what had happened.

"I'm Lambert. Have you found my wife? Hey, Martha, put your head down on the desk." He called a passing technician. "Get someone to take over the switchboard for the rest of the day and ask Mrs. Bancroft if she can come to my office, will you?"

I didn't faint but things blurred for a few minutes. Then I found myself on the couch in Alan's little office with Hope Bancroft holding a bottle of smelling salts under my nose. When I opened my eyes she gave me a glass of water and, at my insistence, let me sit up.

At last Alan said in his big, resonant voice,

"I'd be a fool if I didn't know by now that you've brought me bad news about my wife. That's it, isn't it?"

"We're sorry, Mr. Lambert. She was found about three o'clock this morning in a public parking building. By chance a cop was chasing a couple of muggers. She was in a stolen car and there was no handbag. Nothing at all to indicate who she was. That's why it took so long to get an identification. After lunch today one of the attendants at the morgue thought he recognized her from her pictures, and a few minutes later your call came in to Missing Persons. It's reasonably safe to say the body we have found is Mrs. Lambert's. It agrees with your description in every detail."

Alan took a glass of water from Hope, sipped it, and set it down with a steady hand. "What happened to her?"

"She was mugged and robbed. Knocked on the head and then stabbed twice, probably with an ice pick. Stabbed in the back." Seeing Alan's expression the detective said hastily, "Death must have been very quick, probably instantaneous. I doubt if she ever felt a thing or knew anything about it."

"And not a clue to the bastards who did that?" Alan's voice was held in tight control. "They the muggers your cop was chasing?"

"No, she had been dead for hours by then. From the nature of the stabbing, we've got to assume that it was a dope addict or a mental case. One stab killed her. The second was a vicious action, malignant. But we have no fingerprints, no clue. The only —"

"Go on. I'd rather have it straight out."

"Well, there was one of those little ammonia sprays entangled in the wool of the jacket she was wearing."

"Then she did know what was happening!" I startled them and myself by crying out. "I gave it to her a few weeks ago because she always carried so much currency with her. It amused her, I think. But if she used it that means that she was conscious and perfectly aware of what was happening to her."

"Do you know what jewelry she might have worn?" Saunders asked.

"For God's sake, does that matter now?" Alan exclaimed.

"If it's turned in to a fence, we have a better chance of getting a line on the muggers."

Alan shook his head. "Her maid might know. When I left the house yesterday she was wearing a coral velvet housecoat that made her look more —" He broke off. "That was the last time I saw her, though she telephoned the house and spoke to the butler some time in the early afternoon. He got the message all balled up. He's half deaf and half gaga but Kay — my wife — wouldn't dream of replacing him because he'd been in the family for years. She — was like that."

"We'll talk to the butler and her maid, of course," and Saunders turned to me. "Miss Pelham, do you know what jewelry your sister was likely to be wearing?"

"Her diamond engagement ring and diamond-studded wedding ring, a wrist-watch with a diamond-studded bracelet, a pearl necklace, beautifully matched and quite long, about two hundred pearls I think. She nearly always wore those things unless she was going to play golf or something like that. And she probably had two or three hundred dollars in cash with her."

"That's right. She was Kay Spaulding, wasn't she?"

"She was Mrs. Alan Lambert," Alan said evenly, "and what counts, after all, is how she came to be in a stolen car in a public parking place, who put her there, and why and when she was killed."

"It's rarely easy to establish the exact time of death and it becomes more difficult and uncertain with every passing hour, and last night the temperature dropped sharply, which makes a difference. According to the police surgeon she had been dead between eight and twelve hours when she was found. Her watch stopped at two o'clock."

"Two! You mean my wife was lying unnoticed in a public parking place for that length of time before she was discovered?"

Saunders, who seemed to be the spokesman for the two detectives, said, "It is more than likely that a number of people saw her and cleared out in a hurry so as not to be involved in a murder."

"They might think it a heart attack and believe that something might be done to save her."

"Well," and Saunders sounded apologetic, "that's unlikely as there was a good deal of blood on her wool jacket."

At this moment I noticed that the younger of the two men was watching, entranced, the television screen where Angela was smiling encouragement at a distraught widow whose impending marriage to a second husband was being threatened by a blackmailer.

Saunders noticed it too and called back his companion's straying attention with a sharp word. He looked from Alan to me. "I am sorry but I must ask you to come with me and make an official identification of the body."

Alan got up, dazed but obedient. "Not Martha. It would be too hard on her and it won't be necessary. I'll handle this."

"No," I said, "I'm coming with you."

Hope looked from one to the other but, though she was very pale, she did not remonstrate. "I'll cope here, Alan. Thank God, tomorrow is Saturday and you have no broadcast. Just leave everything to me. And if you can't handle your show on Monday I'll cancel for you and arrange a substitute. But try to give me definite word tomorrow."

"Bless you," he said. "Ready, gentlemen?"

On the television screen a commercial was being done by one of those aggressively comic characters. Outside Alan's small private office people had gathered in little groups in that big bleak room, dark except for its trying brilliant lights, which were not now in use, and where cameras stood idle while *Angela's Affairs* was being shot. They looked around quickly as we came out, but no one ventured to come to us, aghast at the tidings that had filtered somehow through the air. Only Hall Canfield, who had been conferring with the brilliant character actress who was rehearsing for his current play, came to speak to me.

"This is a terrible thing, Mattie. How can I help you?"

I did not attempt to answer him. I just shook my head and went out with Alan, who stared stonily ahead.

I don't think anyone spoke during that ride to the morgue, which was like the pictures one has of it, and unlike, of course, because this was Kay who lay on the table, covered by a sheet. As they drew it back I clutched at Alan's arm, which was like a rock beneath my hand. She was still beautiful, but withdrawn, remote. I had never before realized the finality of death.

"She's different, somehow," I said and then realized that I had spoken aloud.

Saunders answered unexpectedly, "Death's a great disguise." It was only much later that I knew he was, most improbably, quoting Shakespeare.

Alan did not seem to hear him. He stood looking down at the beautiful, still face, his jaw rippling, but otherwise without movement. Only, as the attendant was about to pull up the sheet, he checked him and stretched out his hand, his fingers touching gently a cold cheek. Then, in response to the detective's gesture, he turned obediently toward the door, staggering a little.

I think the most grotesque moment came after we had left her alone in that terrible place. A group of teen-agers on the street recognized Alan and rushed toward him, squealing in excitement. He stared at them, his face blank and unresponsive. It was the detective who, with an imprecation, ordered them out of the way.

Five

No, I assured Saunders, I would be perfectly all right. No, I didn't want to call any of my friends. No, I had no family now that Kay was gone. No, please, I would rather be alone.

Saunders, looking rather troubled, helped me out of the police car in front of the building, attracting a good deal of attention from passers-by who seemed to assume that I was under arrest, especially the woman who had the apartment above mine and watched when I came in and went out. Poor thing, she couldn't have had much to interest her.

"Alan," I began but did not go on. He sat staring at nothing, and was not aware of me.

The first thing I noticed when I unlocked my door was Kay's characteristic scent, fainter than it had been the day before, but still noticeable, because I had put her handkerchief on the table as a reminder to return it.

I wandered around the little apartment, not thinking, not even aware of grief, just stunned by the finality of the thing that had happened, dropping on us like a thunder-bolt. Kay, so beautiful and vital and reck-less, now lying in that cold room.

We had never been close to each other but, in a way, she had been the dominating factor in my life. And all that had ended, ended in a meaningless, stupid manner, be-cause of the rapacity of a mugger, a sub-normal degenerate who killed as casually as a fly climbs the wall.

It must have been about eight when I opened the door to find Hall Canfield standing there, a box of roses under one arm and a big brown paper bag in the other. Wordlessly I stepped back to let him come in.

He looked at me, looked around, and nodded. "I thought so. No one remembered you and what you'd be going through. I'll bet you haven't eaten a bite. No, don't tell me you can't swallow until you've tried."

He went into the kitchen where I heard the refrigerator door open and close and he came back with a glass of Scotch and water in which an ice cube tinkled.

"Drink that and don't try to talk. Please."

Obediently I sipped at the drink while Hall bustled around, put the flowers, long-stemmed yellow roses, in a vase of water and, ignoring my protests, went back to the little kitchen. By the time I had finished the drink he brought me a tray on which there was a bowl of soup and a chicken sandwich, both of which he had brought with him.

"Tuck into that," he said, and stretched out lazily on the lounge chair while I ate. He did not attempt to talk until I had finished every bite. Then he took away the tray and came back to smile down at me.

"There's a little more color in your face now, Mattie."

"You've been terribly kind."

"Would you like to talk about it or would you rather not?"

In a way it would have helped to talk it out but I remembered that Hall had never really liked Kay, though he had admitted that once he had loved her. So I shook my head and he bent over to kiss the top of my head and left. When he was gone I wished I had asked him to stay a little while, to help push back the deadly quiet in the room. When the telephone rang I leaped, startled by the sudden sound, and aware for the first time of the jangling of my nerves.

It was Alan. "Martha, may I come down there for a while? I won't bother you. I just want to be there. You're so restful."

"Come along."

It was longer than I expected before he arrived. As a last resort he had had to escape through the back garden and the basement of a building on the next street to avoid the reporters who were cluttering up the sidewalk outside the Turtle Bay house.

This was an Alan I had never seen before. There was none of his usual control; he could not keep still. When he did not sit with his fingers drumming on the chair arms he paced the floor; his voice, hoarse and strained, went on and on as though he had a talking jag.

He told me how he had first met Kay at the station and how he had been bowled over by her beauty. "The most beautiful woman I have ever seen." But he'd heard about Kay Spaulding, of course, and it never occurred to him to try to see her again. And then she had asked him to lunch the very next day. After that the brakes were off.

"And the miracle is, Martha," he said, his eyes sunken, his face ashen, "that it was the same way with her. Head over heels. Not one man in a million ever has a thing like that happen to him. I should have known it couldn't last. It was — perfect."

He got up again, paced the little room, which seemed smaller than ever with his big figure looming up in it. "I don't suppose you have a drink in the place."

"There's some Scotch," I said, and went out to mix him a drink from the bottle Hall had brought.

"Thanks." He added in some surprise, "This is something new for you, isn't it?" Something like his old friendly grin was on his mouth. "Becoming one of those liberated women now you are on your own?"

"No, Hall brought it tonight, and the roses, and some food because he guessed I wouldn't bother for myself."

"Hall?"

"Hall Canfield."

"One of Kay's discarded suitors." Alan spoke idly and then forgot him. "Sorry to be making a pest of myself but you're the only one who really loved Kay and I couldn't stay home with that damned telephone ringing all the time and the house in a state of siege from reporters, and the police pawing through everything."

"The police!"

"Oh, sure. They wanted to find out what jewelry Kay had been wearing. Maybe they can trace it and in that way get a line on the bastards who killed her. And they wanted to know from Mansfield just what she had said over the telephone, though if they got any sense out of that senile old idiot it's more than I've ever done. And he's worse than ever now. Kay's death seems to have shattered whatever sense he had. He just sits and shakes and when I patted him on the shoulder, as a gesture of sympathy, he leaped in the air and practically yelped. If Kay didn't take care of him, make some adequate provision, I'll do it myself and put the poor beast out to pasture. Someone should have done it a long time ago."

I'd never known him to be so loquacious. He just went on and on.

"I don't see," I admitted, "what difference it would make when Kay called Mansfield."

He shrugged. "For one thing, they are trying to narrow down the time of death."

"But there was her watch, which stopped at two o'clock."

"Yes," he said thoughtfully, "there was that broken watch. Apparently that was someone's mistake. They aren't confiding in me but I gathered that they don't regard the watch as a useful clue, because it seems unlikely anyone would overlook so valuable a piece of jewelry; the thing cost Kay over four thousand dollars. She told me so. As an indication of time of death the police think it's a red herring."

"But why?"

He made a gesture as though asking for

mercy. "I don't know the answers, kid. Ask them."

"Sorry."

He made a grimace that he intended for a smile. "And they wanted to find out if these friends of hers would have — could have —"

"Oh, no, Alan! She didn't know anyone who would be an enemy."

"We are apt to forget that she was a very wealthy woman, kid, because I never cared any more than you did. I told them I didn't know how much she had and I doubted very much whether she did. And then they wanted to know who inherited."

"Alan!"

"I know, but they have to do it. I referred them to her lawyer, Kirk Rhinebold. And then I got the hell out. I hoped you'd put up with me for a while, just until the place quiets down. It's bad enough having to go back and Kay not there —" He ran his fingers through his hair and said in a tone of surprise, "You know, I don't think I can take much more."

"I don't think you can either. Why don't you go to a hotel for the night and let the police know where you are?"

"Can you imagine what would happen if I walked into a hotel lobby now that the news about Kay is out?"

"Okay, then you can sleep on this couch. It opens into a bed. I got it just in case I ever had a friend stay over night."

He was caught by my words and touched my cheek lightly. "You've been lonely, haven't you? Just because you don't complain, people are apt to forget."

"Alone but not lonely. I'm used to it. If you want to stay here you can and I'll give you some sleeping pills Kay gave me once. After that second divorce she had a hard time sleeping." I added, because it was important to say it, "Alan, I'm so glad and so grateful that you made her happy. In a way, I think you gave her all the happiness she ever knew."

He looked at me and made no reply.

So I made up the couch, waited until Alan was through in the bathroom, and put a glass of water and two sleeping pills on the table beside his bed. I found him looking at Kay's handkerchief.

"Why did she come, Martha?"

"I can't imagine. She had never been here since that first visit."

"And no message?"

"You can't lose anything in an apartment this size."

I closed my door and got ready for bed. The spring air was chilly and I pulled up a blanket and thought of Kay, so cold. And at last I cried. Just as I drifted off, I heard the creak of the couch as a sleepless Alan turned over.

II

KAY SPAULDING DIES IN MUGGING

The headlines screamed across the front page. There was a stunning photograph of her taken shortly after her marriage to Alan. There were few details about the mugging, nothing more than I already knew, but the press had made up for a paucity of fact by digging out all their stories about her spectacular marriages and more spectacular divorces, her wild exploits, her recklessness, and, of course, her inheritance of a large block of stock in the Spaulding Copper Company, which made her a very rich woman indeed. Her marriage to Alan Lambert got a lot of attention too.

When he awakened that morning Alan had showered and gone out to get cream for coffee, croissants at a nearby bakery, and to bring back the papers. We ate breakfast in silence, the newspapers tossed onto the unmade couch.

When we had finished Alan said in a

vague tone, "Thanks, Martha, good old stand-by. I don't know what I'd have done without you last night. You helped keep me sane." He gave me a light brotherly kiss on the cheek, squared his shoulders, and went out to face whatever the day might bring.

I was looking out of the window when he went up the steps and out onto the sidewalk, and saw a neighbor, the same woman who had observed my return in a police car the evening before, watch him as he walked down the street, avid curiosity in her face. But it didn't matter, I thought.

That morning, when I had finished with the newspapers and carried them out to the incinerator I made up the couch on which Alan had slept, emptied his overflowing ash-tray, and opened windows to clear the air, heavy with smoke. Alan rarely smoked more than a couple of cigarettes a day as he dared not risk coughing on the job. And I changed the water in the yellow roses, which had opened into full bloom. For the first time I wondered why Hall had come and why he had bothered to see that I ate some supper. Somehow it did not seem like the detached Hall I was accustomed to seeing at the station.

It was nearly noon when there was the sound of heavy, deliberate feet on the steps to the basement and a firm knock at the door. Lieutenant Saunders and his taciturn companion came in. The lieutenant looked around in pleased surprise.

"Well, I wouldn't have thought anyone could do this with a basement. You've got a nice place here, Miss Pelham. Real home-like. What gave you the idea?"

"Well, it was cheap, which was the first consideration, and then it was fun, a kind of challenge, to transform a dark, ugly place into something gay and pretty."

"Cheap? I should think with all that Spaulding money you wouldn't need to think of things like that."

"Oh, I'm not a Spaulding. Kay was only my half-sister, and," I went on quickly, fore-stalling him, "I didn't need to do this, of course. She was always generous about pro-viding me with a home and clothes and — everything. Only I wanted — well, to prove to myself that I could be independent. So Alan got me the job at the broadcasting sta-tion and I found this apartment and fixed it up."

"You didn't move out then because of any trouble with your sister — your half-sister?"

"Trouble?" I repeated blankly and then I remembered the real reason for my leaving the Turtle Bay house and again color burned in my face. "Of course not. Kay and I have never quarreled. Naturally she was upset and hurt about my leaving her house but when she saw this she was delighted with it. She gave me that Renoir as a house gift and it was one of her favorite possessions. She was the most generous —"

"Okay, Miss Pelham. No harm done."

"Have you found out anything more?"

"There's no trace yet of the stolen jewelry or of the money, though the chances are we'll never get that. Her maid said she always carried a lot of twenties in a gold clip. Is that right?"

I nodded. "The clip had her initials in gold and so did the gold pencil and the notebook and engagement book she always carried in her handbag."

"A queer thing —" He let the point drop but when I did not comment he picked it up himself. "The mugger overlooked a watch on a diamond-studded bracelet."

"If she was wearing that bronze wool jacket, that sort of hairy one, the sleeves are awfully wide and might have covered it."

"Still —" He let it drop as though it were of no importance, but I remembered Alan's opinion that the broken watch had a great deal of importance for the police. "Tell me again about that ammonia spray."

I repeated what I had told him the day before.

"How did you happen to have such a thing?"

"I bought it when I realized I'd be coming home alone at night — I've never lived by myself before — and someone told me they are a good thing to have. But when Kay came here and dropped money all over the place I gave it to her. She thought it was funny but she must have tried to use the thing —"

"Oh, she used it, all right." Wilkins spoke for the first time. "It was empty. Someone must have got a full dose of that ammonia."

Saunders gave him a sharp look but Wilkins did not notice.

"I hope so," I said viciously. "But the worst of it is that she knew what was happening when she took out the spray. I wish she hadn't had to know."

"Well, if she marked her attacker it was worth while, and from what I've heard about her she would think so too. I kind of guess she was one who liked to get her own back." Belatedly Wilkins became aware of Saunders' anger and he relapsed into his usual silence.

Saunders settled himself comfortably in his chair and again looked around the room.

"When was the last time you saw your — half-sister?"

"Just a few days ago. She called and asked me to meet her for cocktails at the Plaza after work. But she was here day before yesterday, the day she was killed."

He sat up at that.

"She came while I was at work and she didn't leave a message."

"Then how do you know she was here?"

I picked up her handkerchief, which still lay on the table. "She dropped this — she was always spilling things out of her handbag — and when I came home the room was filled with the scent of her perfume."

He lifted the handkerchief to his nose and sniffed, said, "Ah," and then, after asking my permission, tucked it away in his briefcase. "You have any idea why she came here?"

"None."

"And when you had cocktails she said nothing about planning to visit you?"

"No."

"What did you talk about?"

I thought back. "Nothing important. About my job and some parties she'd been to and a style show she wanted to see and — I don't know. There was nothing special except —"

"What is it, Miss Pelham?"

So I told him about Scott Jameson, about his long friendship with Alan, which Kay had resented because she thought Scott a bad influence, and how she intended to hire a private detective to find out about him.

"Did she?"

"I don't know but she had found out something. She laughed and said she could hardly wait to see Alan's face when she told him what she had found out about his friend. She said he'd get the shock of his life."

"She said nothing else?"

"No, but Hope did." So I told him about Hope Bancroft and her decision to get Scott out of town before he could do any harm to Alan in retaliation for Kay's activities. Hope had given him plane fare and shipped him off to Arizona.

"What made Mrs. Bancroft go to so much trouble? Has she any personal interest in Mr. Lambert's welfare?"

"Not in the way you mean, just in the sense that he is important to the station and she would fight anything that threatened that. As she says herself, it's husband and child to her, and she's a tigress in its defense."

Without transition Saunders asked,

"Who inherits the Spaulding money?"

"I have no idea, though Alan is bound to get a lot, I should think. Kay was so mad about him."

"And you?"

"Well, I haven't thought about it but I suppose there would be something, a token of some kind. I'm not entitled to any Spaulding money, you know. Her lawyer can tell you about it."

"We saw him this morning, Miss Pelham. There is an immense estate and apparently Mrs. Lambert left it in a somewhat confused condition, due in part to her propensity for changing her will every few months and chiefly to the fact that she refused to accept legal advice. There are a number of bequests to friends and servants, which fluctuated each time she drew up a new will. A substantial bequest to her butler, as an old family servant."

"Oh, I'm glad about that! Alan was worried about him and the way the poor old man has taken Kay's death. He's known her all her life, you know."

"Something was certainly wrong when we tried to talk to him last night," Wilkins said and again I saw Saunders' expression. Apparently Wilkins had a genius for speaking at the wrong time, when he spoke at all.

"Couldn't get any sense out of him."

Saunders broke in on Wilkins' revelations. "There was a big bequest for cancer research. It seems her mother died of cancer and she was afraid of it."

"I never knew that! Somehow I can't imagine Kay being afraid of anything."

"Originally," and the detective looked me full in the face, "there was a two hundred and fifty thousand dollar bequest for you" — I gaped at him — "with the comment that you wouldn't know what to do with more than that."

"I should think not," I said rather breathlessly.

"That bequest was put in between marriages, if I can express it like that. Recently she changed her will, cutting your inheritance to twenty-five thousand, because you had caused her pain and humiliation by leaving her home and setting up your own establishment."

When I made no comment he said, "Would you say undue influence had been brought to bear on your sister? That is, your half-sister?"

It occurred to me that he kept repeating that phrase as though it had a great deal of significance. "Good heavens, no! Kay — you'd have to know her to understand. She had all that money at her disposal from the time she was twenty-one and she knew how much power it had. So naturally she came to think of it as a kind of — a kind of —"

"Threat?"

"No, perhaps a way of influencing people."

"Or punishing them?"

I had the queerest stirring of discomfort, a bewildered sense that Lieutenant Saunders was playing games with me. All those questions about whether I had quarreled with my sister — my half-sister, as he carefully corrected himself. The questions about whether I knew what I would inherit, when he knew all the time what the situation was. His suggestion that Kay's having cut my inheritance so drastically would breed resentment. Or more than that?

When I made no reply to his question he went on. "In her most recent will Mrs. Lambert left her husband a half million. If, at sixty, he has not remarried, the full estate comes to him. Naturally her lawyer and the man who handles her estate are considerably upset. Is this about what you would have expected?"

"I've never thought about it at all but I do know that Kay's money was never a factor with Alan. Why it was even Kay who made the advances and brought about the marriage. She told me so herself. And a half million. That's a tremendous lot, isn't it?"

"Not in comparison with the size of the estate. Isn't that clause about remarriage rather tough on a man as young as Lambert?"

"I don't know. I can't judge. And you've got to remember, Lieutenant, that Alan makes a good salary and that he is on the verge of making maybe four times as much. He doesn't need Kay's money."

"The point is, Miss Pelham, that as her husband he is entitled to a certain percentage of it. Of course, he could probably break the will but with an estate as large and complicated as that one it would be a long and expensive process, one that might take years."

I couldn't imagine Alan trying to break Kay's will and to get his hands on more money than she had intended him to have but I did not say so.

Just as I thought he was going to leave, Saunders said, "I'd like to know more about this Scott Jameson."

"I can't tell you anything more. I've never seen him in my life. The only person who knows him, except Alan, of course, is Mrs. Bancroft." And then my hands clutched the arms of my chair. "Do you think Scott had something to do with Kay's death? That it wasn't the mugging it appeared to be? Oh, no!"

He looked at me rather curiously. "Does it matter to you so much who was responsible?"

"Well, of course, it matters! Because if Scott did that to Kay I am responsible. I told Hope that Kay had found out something about the man and she told Scott. She sort of threatened him, to make him go away."

"There's no reason to blame yourself, Miss Pelham." He gave me a paternal pat on the shoulder. "How, by the way, did Mr. Lambert feel about his wife's activities in regard to his friend?"

"She never had a chance to tell him."

"How do you know?"

"Well, I'm sure he didn't know or he'd have said something about it last night."

"That's right," Saunders said smoothly, "Lambert came down to see you last night, didn't he?"

"Yes, he was driven just about mad by the telephone and the reporters and the police pawing through everything. He asked if he could come here and he talked and talked. I've never heard him talk like that before, as though he couldn't stop. About Kay and how beautiful she was and how their marriage had been a perfect thing. He was nearly out of his mind so I suggested he go to a hotel instead of back to his — invaded — house and he said he couldn't face all that curiosity. So then I made up a bed for him on the couch and gave him a couple of sleeping pills and this morning he said it had just about saved his reason."

The detective's eyes rested for a moment on Alan's photograph but he did not mention it. At length, thanking me for my helpfulness, he stood up. And again, at the last moment, he sat down. "By the way, did Mrs. Lambert tell you where she obtained her information about Scott Jameson?"

"I haven't the faintest idea. Oh, God! If I hadn't talked so much —"

"You must not jump at conclusions. If anything occurs to you, let me know, will you?"

And this time he went out followed by Wilkins.

Six

From behind the curtains I watched Lieutenant Saunders and the silent Wilkins come out on the sidewalk. Before they could get into the police car parked at the curb, my first-floor neighbor appeared and I saw her engage Saunders in conversation, or rather she poured out a monologue to which he listened with attention, nodding his head from time to time. From the vindictive look she cast down at my barred window as the car drove off I think she was disappointed that I had not been placed under arrest then and there.

Somehow it had never entered my head that anyone would believe that I could harm Kay, or want to harm her. But my eagle-eyed neighbor had obviously guessed that Alan had spent the night in the apartment and she had drawn her own ugly conclusions. She seemed to believe that on the very day Kay's death was discovered I had launched into an affair with her husband. When I thought of Alan, haggard, overwrought, his hoarse words pouring out unchecked, it made me physically sick.

Now that the detectives had gone I went back over the interview. He had asked odd questions. Although he already knew the contents of Kay's will he had tried to find out what I knew about it, whether I was disappointed or resentful at the cut in my bequest, whether I thought "undue influence" had been brought to bear. Kay's characteristic phrase about the pain and humiliation I had caused her had been taken more literally than it deserved.

He had also tried to sound me out about her fairness in withholding the bulk of her estate from Alan until he was sixty and had not remarried. Well, I had done the best I could for Alan on that score. And then Saunders had looked at Alan's photograph without comment. He had seen my telltale flush when he asked why I had moved out of Kay's house. Was it possible that the man thought I had quarreled with her about Alan, that Alan and I had wanted her to die? Thank God he could not suspect that we had had any hand in her death, having been in full view of any number of people all day long.

With the apartment clean, my clothes in order, and no bills to pay or letters to write, I found myself at a standstill. I could not bear to turn on the television or radio for fear I'd hear something about Kay. I walked the floor until I was tired and then sat staring at nothing.

In mid-afternoon Alan called. "Martha, what is this business about Scott? Saunders has been here telling me Kay had some maggot in her brain about him and says she even hired a detective to check him out. Of all the crazy — did she ever say anything to you about it?"

"Well, you know how she resented him, Alan. She thought he was bad for you."

"But that's absolute nonsense! I haven't a better friend in the world."

"Hope doesn't think so."

"What does Hope know about this?"

I told her that Kay was planning to check on Scott and she said she hoped Scott would never find out because he might — he might — so she gave him the money to fly back to Arizona."

"What the hell! I can't see what right Hope has to meddle. I expect Scott told her where to head in."

"No, she said she really scared him, and she figured there was something he was afraid to have found out."

"Oh, for God's sake! I thought she was a level-headed woman, not the kind to fly off the handle. Just what did Kay tell you about Scott?"

"She said you'd get the shock of your life when she told you what she'd heard about him."

"Nothing more?"

"Nothing more."

"And she didn't produce any evidence to back up this claim?"

"Nothing."

He gave a troubled sigh. "I'd hate to have Scott involved in all this horror. Oh, Martha, the services will be held on Monday morning at ten o'clock. Strictly private. Cremation. Is that all right with you?"

"Yes, I'd prefer it that way."

I came back to my chair, this time to think about Scott Jameson. But there was nothing to go on except for Alan's warm sponsorship. Kay's words that he was bad medicine, and Hope's picture of the man listening to her, his eyes fixed, pushing a ring up and down on his finger while she warned him that Kay would and could expose him.

It was nearly five when Hope came. She looked around, a swift glance of appraisal and surprise. "Why this is charming! It's like you, Martha. Bright and colorful and gay."

I had never felt less like any of these words

and certainly none of them could have applied to her. There were shadows under her eyes, her face was drawn with fatigue, and she looked her full age. She sank into my easy chair with a little sigh of relief. Then she looked at me. "I thought so. No sleep to speak of. What have you been doing? Walking the floor? That isn't going to help Kay or Alan or yourself. Anything new?"

I told her about Alan's plans for a private service on Monday and she nodded agreement. "Let's hope to God no enterprising reporter gets wind of it or the place will be besieged. Alan has enough to bear as it is. At least I've arranged to cover for him on Monday."

"Who's to replace him?"

"You don't replace people like Alan, sweetie. I should think you'd been around enough by now to know that. What I've done is arrange to have Phil Carmichael announce the murder of Alan's wife — not that it will come as news — and hold a symposium with a police inspector, a man from the parole board, and a psychiatrist, on crime prevention. The boss likes the idea and I set it up with Phil's help. I think he has his eye on Alan's spot when he moves over to prime time, and it's not all altruism on his part. Oh, and I've got a temporary switchboard girl to replace you until you are ready to come back. I don't suppose you have a drink in the place."

So again I got out Hall's bottle of Scotch. When I came back with a tall glass, Hope was eying the roses. "At eighteen dollars a dozen those are nice to have. Alan?"

"No, Hall Canfield." I told her how he had appeared the night before with the flowers, the Scotch, the chicken sandwich and soup and had made me eat.

Her brows rose. "Hall? And I thought he was immune to women. How long has this been going on?"

"Nothing is going on. He was just being kind."

"In another ten years," she said dryly, "you'll be less inclined to take people at face value." She sipped thoughtfully. "I understand Hall doesn't want another contract. He's a fool to drop out of sight now while he's in a top bracket. Awards three years running. Unless —" She lighted a cigarette, shook out the match, and looked around for an ashtray. "Unless he has come into money all of a sudden. Did he say anything to you about it?"

"Just that he needed to get some fresh ideas."

"Relying on your inspiration?"

"Oh, nonsense!" I said impatiently.

"I suppose he is taking Kay's death hard. When I said he was immune I meant that she had pretty much made him immune to other women. He was one of her most assiduous escorts for a while, back there when Kay was fancy free. Terribly sunk when she married Alan. I don't think he has ever forgiven Alan for snatching her right out from under his nose."

After thinking it over she said, "I suppose Kay told you about it. I never knew what the trouble between them was."

"No, but then she wouldn't. She didn't boast of her conquests, you know." My voice sounded tart. I had never been less in sympathy with Hope, but whether it was on Kay's account or Hall's, I did not know.

She set down her glass, drew on her cigarette, and said in a reproachful tone, "I suppose you had to tell Alan that I'd interfered about Scott."

"Is he very angry with you?"

"More puzzled than angry, I guess. He says Scott's life is an open book, and if he agreed to go away, it was only because I gave him the impression that that's what Alan wanted. But what really upset him, Martha, is that you told the police about Kay's attitude toward Scott. Saunders came down to the station to see me right after he left you and he turned me inside out. He did the same thing to the whole station. I don't think he believed me when I told him I didn't actually know anything against Scott beyond the fact that he was an inveterate gambler. I just distrusted him. Woman's intuition." Hope grinned at me. "He practically seared me with scorn for that one. And then, after milking the whole station dry, he went up to badger poor Alan, as though he hasn't enough to worry him." She clenched her fist and beat it on the chair arm in exasperation. "I wish to heaven Kay had been more specific with you about Scott."

"I think," I said suddenly, "that's why she came to see me on Thursday. She told me the only other time she came here that if she ever had a secret this was the place to leave it."

"Well," Hope said after a long pause, "it's too late to know now what she had in mind. If anything."

"What on earth did the police expect to find out at the station about Kay? She'd never been in the place but once, the day she met Alan."

"They interviewed everyone they could get hold of. They found out that Alan was well-liked, very popular, in fact, and everyone had a good word to say for him." Hope went on in a different tone, "And they found out that he earns a big salary — a hell of a lot more than they'll ever collect in a lifetime — and expects a much bigger one; that he has no debts and that his financial position is sound; damned good, in fact."

I met her eyes steadily. "I know. I suppose they have to do it but they kept prodding me about Kay's will, about the fact that she had cut me down to a tenth of what she had left me before I moved away from her house. They wanted to know if I resented it. But I — dear God! Hope, they can't possibly think Alan or I could have had a hand in her death. Why even if we had wanted to, it would have been impossible."

"When anyone is loaded the way she was," Hope told me, "people are going to ask questions. They are going to wonder. They are going to speculate. Bound to. Money like that is — well, it's more than the things it can buy; it's power, Martha. That's why the police have to ask. That's why I kept my temper and helped all I could."

"What kind of things did the police want to know, beyond asking about Alan's finances?"

"For one thing how his job worked. Did he just stroll into the station at two o'clock, talk to someone for an hour, and wander off again? That's a bit naive even for a policeman. I told them he was more likely to put in a ten- to twelve-hour day, getting people, reading up on their special interests, all that. I explained that sometimes it takes weeks — months — to get hold of a really important person and arrange a time that is convenient for him. And I pointed out that no program is a one-man deal. Don't people ever notice the long list of credits that accompany the smallest show? I told him it was a combination of cameramen and sound men and producers and technicians of all sorts and sponsors and advertising and men who do most of the writing. I think I finally put it across that a job like that takes work and a whole lot of it."

Hope pressed out her cigarette, finished the Scotch, and shook her head when I offered to refill the glass. "And then," she said deliberately, "the zombie who goes around with Lieutenant Saunders piped up and made the point the other guy had tried to obscure. He wanted to know just when Alan appeared on Thursday and when he left and what he did after that. So I took great pleasure in describing the reception for the unlamented Cosgrave and assured him that Alan had presided over the reception and

97

had been in the full view of at least a hundred bored people whom he had practically bludgeoned into coming to pay their respects to that goon. I never thought I'd be grateful to Cosgrave for anything but at least he did supply an alibi for Alan."

"What do the police really think, Hope?"

"Until they talked to me," she said, "I suspect they thought Scott Jameson was something you had conjured up in your own fertile little brain as a smoke screen, especially after Alan was stupid enough to spend the night here." She touched the photograph of Alan. "You shouldn't be allowed out, Martha, and that's a fact. If I hadn't been able to provide Alan with a cast-iron alibi they'd think the whole thing had been contrived between the two of you, especially as anyone would expect you to be the main legatees in Kay's will. Well, I've had harder problems to tackle than this one, though not much harder, so I guess I can handle this. But no one, no one, is going to wreck things at the station except over my dead body."

I opened the door in response to a tap and found Hall smiling down at me. "Remember me?" When I stood back he saw Hope and for a moment I thought he was taken aback. Then he came in.

There was speculation in the swift look

Hope gave him, but she nodded pleasantly enough as she got to her feet.

"I'm not driving you away, am I?"

"No, I just dropped in for a word with Martha. I have a thousand things to attend to."

"I know. You always have. Those are mighty frail shoulders to carry the whole burden of the station."

"I'm like the woman who ended by carrying a cow. You get used to it."

"And anyhow," and he smiled at her, "you love it."

"And anyhow, I love it." She waved to me and went out.

"I came to take you to dinner and," Hall said, "no back talk. I know a marvelous little French restaurant which hasn't been discovered yet, so it is quiet. And, believe it or not, it's a place where even the waiters wouldn't dream of hurrying you. The idea would shock them to death. Come on. I'll bet you haven't been outside the door today and it's glorious spring weather. Do you good."

He bore down my resistance. "There's nothing to be gained by staying here. Do come along. I'll bring you home early so you can get some sleep. You haven't had much, have you?"

And in spite of my protests I went out into the spring evening, with an opaline sky, and in the west the red ball of the setting sun that seemed to be sliding into the Hudson.

As he started to whistle for a cab I checked him. "Let's walk if it isn't too far."

"Good!" He fell into step beside me and for a block or two he did not attempt to speak, leaving me alone with my thoughts. Once he halted to pick up a small boy on roller skates who had taken a header at his feet; once he steered me around some little girls playing hopscotch on the sidewalk.

"Sure signs that spring has come," he commented.

"Isn't it awfully early for dinner in a good restaurant?"

"Not this particular place," he assured me. "I think you'll like it, Mattie."

There was an unobtrusive sign, Chez Pierre, not more than two dozen tables, widely spaced, with soft lighting but not the murky darkness cultivated by most restaurants. Pierre wanted his customers to see as well as taste his food, and it was worth it.

His wife, a heavily mustached woman, sat at the cashier's desk, working on her accounts, but she looked up alertly when we came in and signaled her husband with a raised eyebrow. Pierre was an excellent testimonial to the quality of his cooking, a stout man with a small mustache above a smiling mouth, and manners that were only a shade too unctuous.

He brought us to a table with the air of triumph of a small tug bringing a liner safe to its mooring, pulled out my chair with tender care, and produced huge handwritten menus with a flourish.

"I hope I didn't drive Mrs. Bancroft away," Hall said at last.

"Oh, I don't think she meant to stay long. She has arranged to have Alan's program handled on Monday while we go to the service for Kay." I explained what she had planned and he nodded.

"Very efficient. She's the most efficient woman I ever knew. I suppose she's a great help to Lambert in getting people for his program."

It seemed to me that Hall was never quite fair to Alan; now he was assuming that much of the credit for his program belonged to Hope.

"Heavens, no! He does all that himself. She doesn't know how he manages it. I heard her call him a living wonder when he captured one of his rare birds."

The petite marmite was delectable and the veal scallopine with Marsala and tiny browned potatoes and peas melted in the mouth. It wasn't until the salad stage that Hall stopped concentrating all his attention on his food and spoke again. "Had a bad time of it, Mattie? No sleep last night? No rest today?"

I told him about Alan spending the night on my couch because he was at the end of his rope, but that, unfortunately, a gossipy neighbor had seen him leave this morning and put the worst possible construction on the incident. The police knew about it too.

Little by little, without intending to do so, simply because his eyes watched me with such a thoughtful, listening expression, I went on until I had told him just about everything I knew. Except for the one important thing, that I was in love with Alan, and somehow I felt sure he had guessed about that.

He was deep in thought while I ate peach melba and drank black coffee and a small brandy. He glanced at the bill and put down what seemed to me an unlikely amount of money. I recalled now, with some chagrin, that there were no prices listed on the menu, but he did not seem to be disturbed and I remembered Hope's speculation that he might have come into some money or at least have some expectations.

Wordlessly Hall steered me toward Fifth Avenue and into a waiting carriage to drive through the park. I'd always wanted to do it and now, with the soft spring breeze on my face, lifting my hair, the lights from the Fifth Avenue apartment buildings bright against the night sky, the muted sound of horns and sirens, and the steady rhythmic clop-clop of the horse, I felt for the moment almost happy. And then I was ashamed of myself, as though, in a way, my contentment was a betrayal of Kay.

At last Hall reached for my hand and held it in a firm clasp. His voice was almost casual when he said, "What it boils down to, Mattie, my dear, is that the police aren't satisfied about the mugging. They are investigating a deliberate murder."

My hand twitched in his but his hold tightened. "So they are going to look for motive: for profit, for hatred, for fear. They are going to pry and probe until there's nothing left hidden in the life of anyone who had any relationship, however slight, with Kay."

He means himself, I thought, but I did not speak.

"It's going to be painful and in the long run it's going to be tragic. Those are tough words, but it's better to accept them now and be prepared for what you're going to be up against. And you won't be alone in this, you know. The last rehearsal was this afternoon and, after the play goes on Tuesday night, I'm going to be a free man. Very much at your disposal."

"What you are really trying to tell me," I said in a small voice, "is that you believe, as Hope does, the police suspect that Alan and I — only —"

"I doubt very much if they are as stupid as that. What I saw of Saunders this afternoon — oh, yes, he talked to me too."

"About Alan?" I was confused.

"No," and his voice was odd, "about Kay. Hope Bancroft seems to have told the police that Alan cut me out with her and that I haven't gotten over it."

"But I thought — you didn't really like her very much."

"No," Hall agreed, "I didn't like her very much."

Seven

Sunday morning the weather turned cold and there was a sprinkling of rain and a sharp wind that was almost like March. I ran across the street to the newspaper stand and came back with the great bulk of *The New York Times* and dumped it on the couch while I fixed breakfast. I had promised Hall to eat properly so I made toast and poached an egg and fixed coffee and some grapefruit and ate it all.

Then I settled down with more coffee and the paper. There were pictures of Kay on inside pages — the story was off the front page by now — and more about Alan than had appeared in Saturday's news. It was all very laudatory, of course, all most cautiously expressed because of the constant danger of libel faced by publishers.

There was information about the funeral service, which was to be private, no flowers, and restricted to the family. There was, fortunately, neither time nor place given for the service, for which I was devoutly thankful. And yet I realized, with a pang, that if Kay had been given a choice she would undoubtedly have opted for a long cortege, a flower-strewn casket, and mobs of people.

The frightening part of the news came in almost reticent fashion. Chief Inspector Bailey, in charge of the case, had confirmed an earlier rumor that the police were not altogether satisfied with the original verdict of death by mugging. At this stage he had no information to give beyond the fact that they were considering "other possibilities." There were certain aspects of the case that left them less than satisfied, and they would naturally explore every possibility. The chief inspector had declined to indicate what the aspects were.

But if the police preferred not to tip their hand, the reporters had been assiduous in exploring every angle of the situation available to them, always, of course, with a wary eye on libel. They had dug up stories about Kay's first two marriages and had hunted down both Bruce Brookfield and John Wentworth. She had divorced Bruce in Reno, charging him with misappropriation of a large amount of money, and Bruce had counter-charged, saying that she had turned the money over to him as a gift at the time of their marriage. What the truth was I never knew but it was like Kay in her careless generosity to endow a bridegroom with a great deal of money and then, when he disappointed her in any way, to strip him of it ruthlessly and even, as in this case, to bring false charges against him.

In any event, Bruce could not be suspected of Kay's murder. At the time of her death and for some time previously he had been living in a considerable degree of grandeur in a magnificent old home in Mexico as the husband of a fabulously wealthy woman old enough to be his mother.

John Wentworth I remembered chiefly as a marvelous dancer. He was also a fine swimmer and he played a good game of tennis. He had been the perfect escort, courteous, attentive, flattering, a handsome host to have at one's disposal. The break-up of that marriage had come because he was an inveterate gambler who ran up huge debts, which Kay had to pay if she was to keep him out of the hands of the goons who control gambling. At length he became too expensive a luxury and Kay divorced him. However, she did give him twenty thousand dollars after the divorce, knowing he had no idea of self-support and no relish for it.

He had, with some difficulty, been discovered in a Miami hotel where he was employed as a gigolo to escort unattached women around the city, to night clubs, and so forth. At the time of Kay's death he had an impeccable alibi but one the reporters refrained from making public.

There was a rehash of all the stories about Kay, her recklessness, and her wild exploits. Whatever she did had always made the news. Pictures had been taken of her with a long-range camera, walking in her garden, nude, at her big house on Long Island, and it was obvious that the reporters lamented being unable to reproduce them.

She had taken up flying and had crash-landed a little plane in an open field where she had nearly killed some farm workers. Later she had recompensed them lavishly, but as one of them had got a serious spinal injury the money did not seem adequate.

In the theatrical section there was a long story about Alan and his spectacular rise in importance from a heavy in Grade B westerns to one of the most respected and influential men in his field. Old interviews were quoted, and the names of some of his more prominent guests given. Accolades from members of the staff of the broadcasting station appeared. He was, they all agreed, a man whose warmth and understanding had made him widely popular in the dog-eat-dog world of competition.

But — and how they had got hold of it so soon I don't know — they knew of Kay's will and that clause about remarriage before Alan was sixty, and the fact that, until then, he was to receive only five hundred thousand dollars. They made this sound like a pittance instead of the fortune it was. And they had got hold of the will of Kay's mother in which she refused to leave anything to her husband in case he should remarry. They also had a lot to say about Kay's frequent change of wills, with bequests fluctuating up and down every few months in accordance with her fleeting moods. Later this bit of information was found to have been divulged by a former law clerk in the firm which handled Kay's affairs, a man who had been fired for incompetence.

The nasty bit was at the end of the story. Mrs. Lambert's bequest to her half-sister, Martha Pelham, had been slashed from a quarter of a million to twenty-five thousand dollars because of the hurt and humiliation she had caused Mrs. Lambert. There was no comment. There didn't need to be. There I was pointed at as a woman with a grievance against Kay.

That Sunday morning I had no attention to give to the news or the editorials or even the book review, to which I usually turned first. I bundled up the papers and took them out to the incinerator. On my way back I encountered my neighbor from upstairs on a similar errand. I was wearing long green velvet culottes, a stunning outfit Kay had given me on my birthday last year. It didn't look much like mourning. My neighbor looked me up and down and brushed past me without a word, making me feel like something out of the last stages of *The Rake's Progress*.

It was awareness of the way I was dressed, which my neighbor obviously found improper, that reminded me that my birthday had come round again. I was twenty-four. It was curious to realize that I was probably the only person in the world who knew — or cared — that it was my birthday. Not, I told myself firmly, that this was any time to think about myself, certainly not to be sorry for myself. If I was going to develop into that kind of woman, the sooner I did something about it the better for all concerned.

So I was taken aback when I opened the door to a messenger who said, "Miss Pelham?" and handed me a big package. He nodded and ran up the steps and I went into the apartment and tore off the wrapping paper. It was a huge box of chocolates tied with a red satin bow. The card fastened to the ribbon said, "Happy birthday, Martha, from Hall."

I was surprised and touched. How like him, I thought, to remember how much any token would mean to me on a day like this. And thinking of Hall I recalled that he disapproved of my staying alone in this basement apartment when there was fresh air and sunshine out of doors. Well, not today, of course, but at least I could take a walk. I changed to a sweater and matching skirt and hunted for a plastic raincoat. I knew perfectly well I had bought it and never taken it out of its plastic envelope. Now where —

I was rummaging for the third time on the shelf of my closet when I heard the tap at the door and went to admit Hall. There was something rather deprecating in his smile when he saw my surprise.

"I know. I know. It's that nuisance again. There's no excuse for barging in like this but I thought I'd just drop around to check up on you. Damned if I know why." He tossed his raincoat over a chair and stared at me in some perplexity. "You're beginning to haunt me, woman. I get worried about you. You need a keeper. No, by George, if it's my allotted job to look after you, I'll marry you," he said manfully.

I ignored this. "Thank you for the candy,

Hall. How nice of you to remember my birthday."

He blinked at me. "Do you always change the subject like that? I talk of marriage; you speak of candy." His eyes fell on the elaborate box with its glossy ribbon bow. He said, "Oh," as though the word had been punched out of him on a sharply expelled breath, and picked up the card. He bent over it for a long time and then he looked at me and all the gaiety had gone from his face.

"When did you get this?"

"Just a few minutes ago."

"Who brought it?"

"Why — you mean you didn't send it?"

"I didn't send it. I didn't know it was your birthday, and I don't," he reminded me, "call you Martha."

"I didn't think of that. Then who —"

"Who was the messenger?"

"I don't know. Just a kid."

"In uniform?"

"No."

"Did he ask you to sign for it?"

"No."

"Well, talk, woman! What did he say?"

"He said," I replied carefully, " 'Miss Pelham?' and put the package into my hands and went away. Period."

"Did you keep the wrappings?"

"Yes, but aren't you being rather absurd about this, Hall?"

He gripped my shoulder so hard he hurt me. "Mattie, did you eat any of the chocolates?"

"In the middle of the morning? Of course not. Oh —"

He nodded. "Exactly."

"But, Hall, this is — ridiculous, isn't it?" I heard my voice trail away. For some reason I was scared. "It may be just a joke or —"

"Or." He slung his raincoat over his shoulder and picked up the box of candy and the wrapping paper.

"You're trying to frighten me," I accused him.

"It's good for you to be frightened. It might make you a little more careful, more watchful. I don't know what this is all about so don't try to prod me, but I don't like any part of it."

"But there's no reason why anyone would —" As he started for the door I demanded, "Hall, what are you going to do? You've got to tell me."

"I'm going to take this to a pharmacist I know and find out if anyone tampered with the candy. He's a guy I can trust. I asked him for information about poisons once when I was doing a play and we got to be friends;

play chess together every couple of weeks. You'll like him, Mattie. He's quiet appearing and has a nice, unexpected, irreverent sense of humor. We'll all have dinner together some night."

"But what are you going to tell him?"

"I'm just going to ask him to make an analysis. And don't worry. No problem. He'll check and then keep his mouth shut. So that's all right."

"I'm going with you." As Hall hesitated I said, "After all, I'm the one who is most concerned in this. And I was going for a walk anyhow. I was just looking for my raincoat when you came."

"You won't need it. The rain has stopped. Okay, come along." It was not a particularly gracious invitation but I went along anyhow.

Hall's friend was a slight young man with a deeply furrowed forehead and buck teeth. He was behind the prescription counter, wearing a white jacket, and listening patiently to a voluble woman who was retailing her symptoms in a hoarse voice. At length he said firmly, "Sorry, madam, I cannot recommend any medicine for you."

"What are you here for, young man?"

"There's a strong chance of some infection. You should consult a doctor. Then —"

"Doctors!" she snorted. "What I want —"

In his quiet way he was adamant and at length she went out, presumably in search of a doctor, no easy task on a Sunday morning.

The young pharmacist looked over his glasses at Hall and grinned when his eyes fell on the box of chocolates. "For me? This is so sudden."

"It might have been," Hall said dryly. "Take a look at these, will you, Ben? But don't taste them."

"Another play?"

"Somehow I don't think this is fun and games." His voice made the pharmacist look at him with a startled expression. "Mattie, this is Ben Forbes, the best pharmacist and the worst chess player I know."

"That," Forbes assured me, "is slander."

"Of course it is. And jealousy too, probably."

"And this is Martha Pelham." Hall caught Ben's eyes. "Mrs. Alan Lambert's half-sister."

After a moment's hesitation the pharmacist reached over and took the package out of Hall's hands.

"Keep the wrapping paper," Hall instructed him, "just in case."

"I can't do this right away. I have a number of prescriptions to fill."

"Half an hour?"

"Have a heart, man!" He glanced at the clock. "Make it one o'clock. But no later. I go out to lunch then."

"Fine. We'll collect you and have lunch together. That all right with you, Mattie?"

It was rather a high-handed way of doing things, making plans and consulting me when he had a *fait accompli* but I nodded and we went out of the drugstore, past the soda fountain at which people were having late breakfasts or early lunches, past the counter with its perfumes and cosmetics, past the shelves devoted to clocks and watches, past the tobacco and candy counters, past the revolving shelves of books and the loaded shelves of toothpastes, mouthwashes, pills for nonsleepers and those who want to keep awake, pills for those who weigh too much or too little, and all the miracle workers to keep men virile and women desirable, and, above all, to hold back the encroachment of old age.

We walked up Fifth Avenue, nearly deserted on a Sunday morning, looked in shop windows, sauntering toward Central Park. It was safe enough by daylight at the southern tip, too early for young lovers to lie on the damp grass, and too chilly for elderly men to play checkers on one of the benches. Even the balloon man was not in evidence as the early rain had discouraged children from playing.

When I found that Hall steadily refused to answer my bombardment of questions I fell silent and then, provokingly, he began to talk.

"Read the papers?"

"The *Times*. The police don't really believe Kay was mugged, do they?"

"Somehow it never seemed likely to me," he admitted. "I told you once she was the kind of person to whom things happen but not — how can I put it? — accidentally. And, no matter how loyal you are, Mattie, you are honest enough to admit that she made a lot of enemies."

"People who stab in the back — literally stab?"

"Murderers don't follow the rules of civilized behavior."

"I know that, but — Hall, I think Lieutenant Saunders had a kind of idea that I was — involved with Alan."

"Well, aren't you?" He said it so gently that it was a moment before I grasped his meaning. He watched sympathetically my struggle to find adequate words. "Look, Mattie, even a blind fool would know that you think you are in love with Alan. Wait!" as I jerked my arm away from his hand, "I don't believe for a moment there is anything wrong about the situation. He's just one of those men who are irresistible to women. God knows why! He's an ugly devil. Evidently it's something women can't help, except," and he took my arm again, holding it firmly, "that you did help it, didn't you, when you moved out of his orbit and into that little apartment of yours."

I didn't find any answer to that.

"Angry?" he asked at last.

"I don't know," I admitted.

At one o'clock, feeling the better for the walk, I accompanied Hall to the pharmacy where his friend Ben was waiting for us, a man who looked so sober that Hall grasped my hand firmly in his own and gave it a comforting — and warning — squeeze before he released it.

He steered us to a restaurant and, without referring to Ben for his choice, by which I realized how well they knew each other, he ordered a Bloody Mary for him, dry sherry for me, and a martini for himself.

It was only when the drinks arrived, had been sampled, and lunch ordered, that Hall said, "Okay, Ben. Let's have it. I take it the news is bad."

"Strychnine."

"God!"

At Hall's insistence I finished my drink but I couldn't swallow my lunch. It tasted of ashes.

"But there's nobody," I kept insisting, "there's nobody who would do that to me."

"I ought to report this," Ben said to Hall.

And Hall, to my astonishment, agreed. "We'll do it together. This is no time to be coy. Ice picks and strychnine! I'll call Lieutenant Saunders when we leave here. Is there anyone to replace you if you're asked to come and give your evidence in person?"

"There are always three of us on duty. And in a case as urgent as this the rules don't apply anyhow."

Hall pushed back his chair. "I'm going to call the police now. Okay with you?"

When he had gone his friend gave me rather a wintery smile. "Knowing Hall has its grimmer aspects." He added, seeing my expression, "He's a good friend, you know. And at least you didn't sample any of the chocolates."

"No, I didn't." But it was not much comfort. "Why? Why? What have I done?"

Naturally Ben had no answer to that.

Hall came back to the table. "Saunders is out on another case but his laconic friend Wilkins is coming to meet us at the pharmacy in twenty minutes." He finished his coffee. Abruptly he asked me, "Look here, Mattie, has Scott Jameson any reason to be gunning for you?"

"For me!"

"You do sound like an idiot child," he remarked with detachment. "Yes, for you. Are you sure Hope Bancroft actually put him on the plane or did she just buy him a ticket and hope for the best?"

Eight

Wilkins came into the pharmacy, accompanied by a bulky man in plain clothes who couldn't possibly have been anything but a policeman. I introduced them to Hall who took them back to talk to Ben. The four men went into a back room to confer, leaving me alone, which infuriated me. After all, I was the one most strongly concerned, wasn't I? I was the one who had got the poisoned chocolates. I was the one someone wanted dead.

But when I had framed that thought in my mind I stopped resenting being ignored and realized I was frightened.

At length the men emerged from that back-room conference, Ben resumed his place behind the prescription counter and the two detectives, accompanied by Hall, came up to me. The bulkier of the two men, whose name was Fischer, was carrying the candy box and the wrappings.

"We'd like you to make a statement, Miss Pelham," Wilkins said. He looked around the busy pharmacy.

"Let's go back to my apartment. It's only

a couple of blocks."

So we went back to the apartment, Hall and I on foot, the two detectives drawing up at the curb in the police car as we reached the house. I noticed that my neighbour, as usual, was stationed at her window and saw my arrival followed by a police car. She was really having a field day.

When I had finished my story and Fischer had taken it down laboriously, the pen seeming too small for his massive hand, Wilkins asked me to tell it all over again. He tried to get a description of the messenger, who might have been anyone. Young. No uniform. I hadn't noticed what he looked like so I couldn't identify him. Not possibly.

Wilkins turned to Hall who explained that he had not sent the candy. He had not known it was my birthday, and he didn't call me Martha. It was just chance that he had happened to drop in that morning. Aware, perhaps, of a certain skepticism in Wilkins's face he said, "And I didn't come to see how strychnine agrees with Miss Pelham's constitution."

Wilkins eyed him thoughtfully. "Hall Canfield? You write up stories for television, don't you?"

"I write plays."

"Same thing. What made you decide to

quit all of a sudden?"

"How did you get hold of that?"

"Oh, these things get around," Wilkins said vaguely.

"I needed a change. I want to pick up some new ideas. I'm getting stale."

"Come into some money?" Wilkins asked.

"No, I —" Hall broke off, his face hardening. "What is that supposed to mean?"

Wilkins shrugged. "Just that it takes money to retire — at your age."

"I'm not retiring and I've been earning damned good money these past five years."

"Why would anyone who wanted to poison Miss Pelham make use of your name?"

"That's what I intend to find out."

"You are old friends, aren't you?"

"No, we've known each other only a few weeks."

"That's right. It was Mrs. Lambert whom you knew so well, wasn't it? I saw something about it in one of those columns once. 'Kay Spaulding's current flame.' Something like that, wasn't it?"

"I don't," Hall said curtly, "read gossip columns," but I didn't feel that he came off too well.

"Just for the record, as a matter of routine," Wilkins asked, "where were you on Thursday, Mr. Canfield, say from noon until eight o'clock?"

"Thursday?" Hall's eyes narrowed. "Oh, of course. That's when Kay was killed. Well — let's see. I went to the station about ten because I'd had to rewrite a bit of dialogue and wanted to see how it went. Timing and all that. It went well so I didn't stay, as the rehearsals have been going smoothly and the director is good at his job. I went to Abercrombie's to get some fishing tackle as I was planning to take some time off. I am still," he added challengingly, "planning to take some time off." When Wilkins declined to pick up the gauntlet he went on, "Abercrombie will probably have a record of the sale because I have a charge account there. Then I went to the Yale Club for lunch."

"Meet anyone?"

"I lunched alone. I probably saw at least a couple of people I know but I don't remember anyone in particular. Then I walked over to the Forty-second Street Library to look up some material, I worked in the cardroom for about forty minutes or so, picked up my books, and made a few notes. I left there about half-past four, walked home, mixed myself a couple of drinks, and had dinner at a big Italian restaurant on

Forty-eighth Street —"

"Alone?"

"Alone," Hall said evenly. "Then I went to that new Shakespeare production and, if you care to know, it stinks. Nothing indicates the indestructible greatness of Shakespeare better than the amount of abuse he can take and still survive. After that I went home to bed." He added sweetly, "Alone."

Wilkins turned to me then. "Have you often felt that you were being persecuted, Miss Pelham?"

I stared at him, bewildered, and then I was angry. "Why? Do you think I made this up? Do you think I sent myself those poisoned chocolates? And, if I had, would I have involved Mr. Canfield, who has nothing to do with me anyhow? Just the merest acquaintance."

I thought Hall looked amused but he was watchful, studying Wilkins's attitude, puzzled by it.

"What did Mrs. Lambert tell you about the man Scott Jameson?" Wilkins's mind jumped around like a flea.

I repeated the little I knew. He hammered at me. There must be something more. Why had Kay come to my apartment when I was gone? I didn't know. She had not done so before?

"There wouldn't have been any sense in it when she knew I was at work."

"How did she get in? Did you give her a key?"

I shook my head. At a gesture from Wilkins, the big man, Fischer, went out of the room. It was some time before he came back, during which Wilkins fell into his usual silence and said nothing at all, until I was half frantic and even Hall was showing signs of restlessness.

"The super handles five buildings in the block," Fischer reported when he returned. "He was repairing a washing machine down the street, reason it took so long to find him. He admitted Mrs. Lambert to this apartment as soon as she identified herself as Miss Pelham's sister. He remembers her because she was so beautiful and came in a Mercedes, which she was driving herself. She also tipped him five dollars to let her in."

"Did she explain why she was coming when her sister wasn't there?"

"She said she just wanted to leave a message. And she wasn't inside more than five minutes because he saw her come out again and drive away. About half-past twelve he thinks it was. He said she wasn't carrying any package, anything like that. She had nothing with her but a handbag."

"Did she leave a message?" Wilkins asked me.

"No, she didn't. I've looked everywhere."

Wilkins got up. "Fischer will transcribe his notes and I'd appreciate it if you'd come to the station later this afternoon to read and sign them if they agree with your impression of this interview." He nodded to Hall and the two detectives went out, while I stared blankly after them.

"They didn't believe me," I said at length.

"No," Hall agreed, "they didn't believe you. They didn't believe me either, so we're in the same boat."

"Not quite," I pointed out. "At least no one wants you to be dead."

When the telephone rang I jumped nervously. It was Alan. "Martha?" He sounded relieved. "Thank God! I was getting worried about you. I must have called half a dozen times."

I couldn't tell him the whole ugly story over the telephone so I said, "Hall came and took me for a long walk and then we had lunch. But — I'd like to see you, Alan."

"Hall?" he said in surprise. Then, "I want to see you, too. Something damned funny has been going on. That's why I was so worried when I couldn't get you. I'd appreciate it a lot if you could come up here. It's not that I'm unwilling to come to you but the — well, call it evidence — is here."

"Why, of course I'll come. Right away if you like."

"You never fail, do you, Martha? Bless you."

When I explained to Hall he said, "Something funny going on? I'm coming with you."

"Why?" I didn't mean to be discourteous; I was just surprised.

"I don't like the way things are happening."

"Neither do I," I said feelingly. "I'll have to change my clothes. If I'm going to Kay's house, I'll have to wear a black dress. I don't care about these things but other people do and it might seem disrespectful or something."

"Take your time. I'm in no hurry." Hall settled himself in his favorite lounge chair. " 'I have no precious time at all to spend,/ Nor services to do till you require.' "

I looked at him in surprise and he smiled blandly. "Shakespeare, my pet. Just a touch of culture to sweeten the day." But there was a challenge in his eyes which I ignored.

When I came out in the only black dress I owned, Hall shook his head. "You should always wear bright colors. Black submerges you."

This time I made no objection when he called a taxi; I had had my fill of walking for one day. Mansfield opened the door, looking as though he had aged since I saw him only a few weeks before.

"Mr. Lambert is in the library, Miss Pelham. He's expecting you." The old butler spoke in a hushed tone and there was a quaver in his voice. I didn't know whether it was grief for Kay or anxiety over his own future, though I was almost positive that she had left him a sufficient income to live on, for, of course, Alan would not be keeping up this big house now that he was alone, and, in any case, he found Mansfield's doddering ways exasperating, for which I could hardly blame him. It was increasingly difficult for him to report a telephone message accurately. He admitted people whom Kay did not want to see and refused her to people whom she wanted to see.

Mansfield smiled at Hall. "It is a long time since you have been here, Mr. Canfield," and again I was aware that, in the not too distant past, Hall had known Kay very well indeed. The wonder was that I had never encountered him until we had met at the station, but I had spent one whole winter studying art in Boston and I had been away until I discovered I was not good enough ever to get out of the amateur class.

"I just don't see how it could have happened," Mansfield said. "I checked the locks last night just as I always do. But I guess I'm getting a little old and forgetful and hard of hearing. And, of course, the staff sleeps on the fifth floor. It's a well-built house, Miss Pelham," and he glanced uncertainly at Hall, "I'd like to speak to you, if I may."

"Why, of course."

From the top of the stairs I heard Alan call, "That you, Martha? Come on up, will you?"

"I'll see you before I leave," I promised Mansfield.

Hall and I met Alan at the top of the stairs. He came to give me a hug and, in some surprise, he shook hands with Hall. "Good of you to come, Canfield, but I'm afraid I haven't time today to talk." With an apologetic smile and a slight gesture he dismissed Hall who, apparently unaware, stood his ground.

"Something damned queer has happened," Alan told me. "Someone got into the house late last night or early this morning and practically tore Kay's rooms apart, her little boudoir and her bedroom and bath and the room on the first floor where she wrote letters, made out menus, and all that."

"Was anything taken?"

He shrugged. "That's why I wanted you, Martha. She had so much stuff that I wouldn't know the half of it; and I thought you could tell what's missing before I inform the police. That's why I was so upset when I tried to get you and there was no answer."

So then I told him about the chocolates that were supposed to be from Hall, whose opportune arrival had prevented me from eating any of them, and how Hall's friend in the pharmacy had found strychnine in them, and that we'd turned the whole thing over to the police.

Alan stared at me, his eyes sunken, his mouth twitching, and I realized with a pang of pity how he had aged since Kay's horrible death.

"My God," he said softly. "Oh, my God! What's going on here? As though someone were trying to wipe us all out." He turned to Hall then. "I don't get your position in all this."

"I don't either, but if someone is taking my name in vain I'm damned well going to find out who it is. You say you haven't called the police yet about what happened here?"

"I thought it would be better to know just what the situation is before I do and I wanted to have a list of missing articles — if anything is missing."

"How about Kay's maid?"

"Kay?" Alan's brows arched.

"Hall is an old friend of Kay's," I explained.

"Oh, of course, so he is. I'd forgotten. Well, about the maid. Of all damned fool things to happen, she began cutting a wisdom tooth — at her age! — and had to go to an orthodontist yesterday to have it cut out. She'll be in the hospital until tomorrow. Martha, do you mind going up and looking through her things? I warn you the place is in a mess."

"The trouble is that I don't really know what she had."

"You'll do your best. I hate to push this onto your shoulders. After that box of poisoned candy — Good God! — you've had enough for one day. But somehow I can't bring myself to go back there if I can help it."

I nodded and went up to the third floor. Kay's rooms were at the back, with a view over the garden to the East River. She had a little sitting room, with Louis XV furnishings, draperies, and satins, a delicate jewel of a room, permeated with her scent.

At first glance nothing seemed to be out of order, but the drawer in an exquisitely carved and painted table was a jumble of papers. I did not attempt to sort them out, as I did not know what should have been there, and anyhow, whether she was dead or not, I had no right to go through her private papers.

In her bedroom with its tufted satin headboard and the footboard heavily carved, with its long closet where dresses and suits and coats hung on scented hangers, matching shoes below, hat boxes above, I stopped in dismay. Dresses and coats had been flung on the bed, the pockets of coats and of a couple of trouser suits were turned inside out, drawers emptied on the floor and their contents in an unholy mess.

There was a safe built into the base of the bed, a clever affair Kay had once showed me with the delight of a child displaying a new toy. Here she kept her important jewelry: a diamond necklace and some emeralds which were supposed to be priceless, rings, earrings, a bracelet, and a few private papers. She had told me the combination then

— it was concealed in the scrollwork in the carving — in case anything happened to her.

"You're the only human being I have ever completely trusted," she had told me then. That was seven years ago, and I was not sure that I could remember the combination after all that time. It had been something childishly simple, I was sure of that. I sat down on the floor and studied the carving. Then I noticed the Old English letters and remembered the combination spelled M A R T H A.

I spun the dial right, left, right, left, right and as I turned the knob the little safe opened under my hand. Inside were stacked the familiar jewel cases: the emeralds, the diamond necklace, and a number of pieces I had forgotten, were all there. I reached tentatively for the papers: a copy of her most recent will, a long list of her stocks, several bank books, a thick bundle labeled: Spaulding Copper, and a page torn from a notebook on which Kay had scrawled: "S. J. Landlord at apartment. Get pictures if possible. See Martha."

After a moment's hesitation I removed this memorandum and closed and reset the safe. Then I went through the bathroom where the same chaos existed.

At last I went down to the second floor

where Alan was still sitting at the desk in the library. Apparently he had succeeded in dislodging Hall. In Kay's little room at the back of the house on the first floor I found her desk in the same disorder that had reigned above. Papers were scattered all over and her desk drawers were a jumble. The room was still scented with her perfume and I could see her sitting there, her face glowing, telling me about her stunning new husband and her happiness. And a few weeks later she lay on a table in the morgue and Alan, his face bleak and aged, sat alone in the library, his world shattered.

I didn't even know that I was crying until Mansfield came creaking into the room and set beside me a tray with tea and cinnamon toast, and cloves stuck in the slice of lemon the way I liked it. There was even my favorite crystalized ginger on the saucer.

I couldn't control my voice so I just put my hand on his and squeezed it. When he had poured the tea I asked him about the telephone call he had taken from Kay the day she was killed. Only three days ago!

He shook his head hopelessly. "I've thought and thought about it and, of course, the police have asked me. But I couldn't tell them anything. I'm getting a bit hard of hearing and I couldn't catch the name of the people madam was meeting." He wasn't even sure of the time of her call but thought it was about twelve-thirty. But that meant that she had called from my apartment, which made no sense at all. Anyhow, now that I thought about it calmly, it was unlike Kay to call home to explain a casual encounter, particularly as Alan would not be back until late, in any case.

"Are you sure it was Mrs. Lambert's voice?"

Mansfield looked like a dog who expects to be scolded. "I never really questioned it. I took it for granted. It was sort of high like hers."

"Never mind, Mansfield, you aren't to blame." As he started out of the room I said, "I suppose Mrs. Lambert was as usual that morning."

"Oh, yes. Laughing. Joan, her maid, heard her laughing when Mr. Lambert went in to say good morning, as he always did. High spirits, Joan said, madam, that is, Mrs. Lambert was in. That made me feel better, knowing she had been gay like that on her last day because —" He broke off. "That's the doorbell. People are mighty inconsiderate," and he went creaking out of the room.

The tea helped a lot and I had regained control and powdered my nose to hide

136

traces of tears when I went back up the stairs to Alan. He looked at me quickly. Evidently I had not been as successful as I had thought about concealing the tears. He stretched out his hand to me. "Poor Martha. Did I give you a horrible job?"

"I can't understand it. Obviously someone ransacked the place looking for something."

"But what, in heaven's name, can it be?"

"I don't know. Certainly not her jewelry. That's all there."

"It is?"

"Didn't she ever show you her safe?"

"Why no."

"It's concealed in the foot of that big carved bed of hers. Old English letters. The combination is M A R T H A. Right, left, right, left, right. Her jewelry is there, all of it, so far as I know, and her Spaulding stock, and a list of shares, and her will and — this." I handed him the memorandum from her notebook and he read it, frowning. "Though what it's supposed to mean — and why she put it in her safe —" After a moment I said the obvious. "It looks as though she had discovered Scott Jameson's address."

He gave a long sigh. "Poor girl! Poor foolish girl!"

"Just the same," I told him, "it would be nice to know where Scott Jameson is now. And," I added defiantly, "where he was on Thursday."

"I'll find out, Martha. Scott wouldn't lie to me. And there's one thing sure. He couldn't break into this house and, if he did, he wouldn't know which rooms Kay used. He's never been inside the place."

"How could anyone break in?"

"God knows. The simplest explanation is that Mansfield forgot to lock up. Kay had a key, I have one, and Mansfield has one. Have you your key to the house, Martha?"

"I suppose so but I don't know where it is." I pulled my apartment key out of my handbag. "That's the only one I carry now."

"But someone could have taken yours?"

"I don't see how."

"I don't like it," Alan said suddenly. "I don't like it at all. Someone has murdered Kay, brutally, viciously, and someone sent you poisoned candy. Well, there's one thing sure. You aren't going to stay alone in that apartment of yours any more, not until we find out what this is all about. Pack a bag and come up here to your old room, Martha. Come where I can keep an eye on you."

When I hesitated he said in surprise, "Why not? Certainly that's the sensible thing to do."

I couldn't think of any easy way of telling him that the police half suspected an emotional bond between Alan and me, but there was no help for it so I blurted it out.

"So you see if I moved back into the house as soon as Kay — is out of it —"

"I see." After a moment Alan said in a matter-of-fact tone, "Well, we can't have that, of course. But, at least, do one thing to ease my mind, Martha, like a good girl. Go to a hotel at least for tonight." He reached in his pocket. "Let me pay for it. No, I insist. After all, it's for my peace of mind. Later, after the service tomorrow, we can talk and maybe think a little more clearly. But just for tonight —"

He was so much in earnest that I promised I wouldn't spend the night alone again without telling him.

As I prepared to leave he walked down the stairs to the door. "There will be a lot to attend to. Of course, I'll stay on here for a while, at least, as I don't know what Kay wanted done about the house and the furniture and the servants, all that. And thank God for Hope! She will cover for me tomorrow, and the next day —"

"You aren't planning to go back to work at once!"

"It's my job. But the rest of the week will be easy. People I arranged with some time ago and at least three of them each day so, if one dries up, the talk can keep going without too much help from me."

"You're — quite a guy, Alan."

He patted my shoulder. "Oh, I forgot to tell you that your friend Canfield had an errand. He said he'd come back for you." He grinned. "You've picked up quite a watchdog but watch your step, honey. Big bad wolves don't always show their teeth, you know."

I laughed at the idea of Hall being a wolf, and on that more cheerful note I left him.

Nine

When I left the Turtle Bay house I found Hall waiting for me on the curb where he was giving a light to a man with graying hair and sloping shoulders. Hall came toward me and the man walked off. He had a curious walk, his knees bending exaggeratedly at each step so that his walk had a kind of spring or bounce in it.

"Alan said you had an errand. You didn't need to come back, you know."

"No problem. I'm free as the air. Anyhow, I'm in this thing, Mattie, if only because someone used my name in sending you that candy." He whistled for a cab.

"Where are we going?" I asked suspiciously and he grinned at me.

"Haven't you forgotten that you have a pressing date with the police when you sign that statement you made?"

This time Saunders was the one who handed me my statement, let me read it through in silence, and then sign my name. He evidently expected me to get out in a hurry but I sat where I was. "Something very queer, very frightening, has happened."

"That business of the poisoned candy? We're looking into it, Miss Pelham. I don't need to tell you to be very careful in case anything else — not that I think there is any danger of a second attempt."

"There's been some kind of attempt," I said, and told him about the ransacking of Kay's rooms in the Turtle Bay house. "They were just taken apart. Someone must have been searching for something small, so small that it could go in a pocket, because the pockets in her coats and slacks had been pulled inside out. All the drawers had been dumped out and the stuff just scattered, not only in her rooms upstairs but in the little room on the first floor which she used for writing letters."

"When did all this happen?"

"Alan doesn't know. Either late last night or early this morning. He called and asked me to go through her things and see what was missing, but of course I don't know just what she had. All I'm sure of is that whoever it was did not tamper with her safe." I told him about the combination lock and how, seven years ago, Kay had showed me the safe and told me the combination, saying that someone ought to know in case of her death and that I was the only one she trusted.

"She said you were the only one she trusted?" Saunders asked sharply.

"Well, that was long before she married Alan; in fact, it was just after her first divorce, when she wasn't very trustful of anyone."

"Did you look in the safe?"

I told him what I had found: the jewelry, intact so far as I knew; the list of her stocks; bankbooks; Spaulding papers in a thick bundle; and along with her will the little memorandum torn from her notebook.

That interested him. "Where is it?" He held out his hand.

"I gave it to Alan. And I'm just about positive that S.J. means Scott Jameson and Kay had found out somehow where the man lives."

Saunders drummed thick fingers on his desk, shoved a rather smelly ashtray out of the way, looked at me from under bushy eyebrows. "And what explanation has Mr. Lambert to give for the fact that he has failed to notify the police about this ransacking of his house, particularly when it follows the murder of his wife?" He looked at his watch. "He's had a whole day to do it in."

"He wanted to wait until I had had a chance to check and see whether anything was missing so he'd have something concrete to give the police and then he couldn't reach me for hours. I'd got the poisoned chocolates and Mr. Canfield and I had taken them to the drugstore and then called you and we'd taken a long walk and everything so it was hours before Alan could reach me."

"Thank you, Miss Pelham." Saunders stood up, dismissing me, and gave Hall a queer, questioning look.

"I'm looking after her," Hall said and escorted me out of the station and into the pale dusk of a spring day. The air was curiously light and just faintly tinged with the excitement of the new season, which one feels, even in the heart of Manhattan, above the fumes of exhaust and the sound of trucks rumbling and the restless beat of the feet of people swarming home from work.

When we came out of the police station a man who had been standing beside a taxi talking to the driver got in. He had graying hair and something about the slope of his shoulders was familiar. I tugged at Hall's arm but he did not notice it until he had put me into a cab and given an address.

"Hall," I said then, "that man was standing outside Kay's house when we left. He's the man who asked you for a light."

"Oh?"

"Hall." I pulled his sleeve again. "It's rather a coincidence, isn't it? Do you think he is following me?" And, hearing my own words, I said, "That's what Sergeant Wilkins meant, isn't it? That I have a persecution complex? But I haven't. Honestly I haven't."

"Of course you haven't." He captured my clutching hand and held it firmly, less to comfort me, I thought, than to prevent me from wrinkling his beautifully cut jacket. When he came to see me, I noticed in satisfaction, Hall abandoned his slovenly ways and dressed in his best bib and tucker. "I'm keeping an eye on you from now on. No one is going to have a chance to bother you. Get that?"

"I get it. Only it's not very practical, is it? You can't be with me all the time."

"I can damned well try. And if it has too bad an effect on my reputation you'll just have to make an honest man of me."

"Oh, don't be silly. Hall —" My voice was so small he had to bend over to hear the words. "Do you think that man could be Scott?"

He looked startled. Then he said thoughtfully, "Scott seems to keep reappearing in this business, doesn't he?"

"Yes, he does, and — hey, where are we? Where are you taking me?"

The taxi had stopped in front of the Beekman Towers. "Come along, Mattie."

"But —"

"No lip from you, kid." He paid off the cabbie and steered me into the building. "We are now going up to the roof and have a drink, or two drinks, maybe even three drinks, depending on circumstances. We will look out at the lights of New York from a great height and think pleasant thoughts — or, better still, not think at all. And then we will descend to my apartment — yes, I have a small apartment here — and order dinner sent up. We will eat in peace, not bothered by the noise of a restaurant or the curiosity of diners. We will then —"

"It seems to me that for several days you have done nothing but buy me meals."

"My pleasure," he said politely.

"But really, Hall —"

"Really. Have you a better plan? You've got to eat. After that, we'll discuss the next step."

I eyed him warily but there was nothing to be read in his face but a kind of mischievous challenge, which I thought it better to ignore.

We got off the elevator on the roof, stood for a few minutes watching the lights of New York and Long Island come on and then took a table by the window where Hall, who was obviously well known here, ordered for us and reached absently for a dish of salted peanuts, which he began to nibble.

He stuck firmly to what he referred to as his scenario. We talked little over cocktails — we stopped at two — and watched the lights and occasionally made an idle comment that had no bearing on the horrible things that had been happening or the service to be gone through the following morning when Kay's beautiful body was — I resolutely withdrew my thoughts from the unthinkable, the unbearable, and listened to Hall's light talk about nothing in particular.

Later we had dinner in his apartment, a few floors lower down. There was a living room with deep, comfortable chairs and good reading lamps and a really magnificent record player with an impressive collection of records. Beyond, there were two bedrooms on the front of the building, again with that stupendous view. One of them had rather a spartan appearance but the other had been transformed into a workroom, with a big desk, a covered typewriter swung out on hinges at one side, filing cases, and the walls lined from floor to ceiling with bookshelves.

Hall grinned as he showed them to me. "The management raised hell," he said cheerfully, "until I promised — in writing — to have them removed at my expense and the walls repainted when I give this up. Not that I expect to. It's quiet, which is something in New York, and convenient for most things, and there are some good restaurants within walking distance. What more could any man want?" He eyed me, again with that mischievous challenge. "Unless, of course he should change his status."

I made no answer to that, which amused him. At his suggestion we ate steaks and baked potatoes and a salad, though I balked at dessert. It was over dinner, wheeled in on a table from the restaurant downstairs, that I told him about my promise to Alan not to spend a night alone for the present, at least not without telling him.

"So what are you going to do?"

I thought I saw a proposition looming in his eyes so I said hastily, "I'm going to a hotel tonight. I'll just go back and pack a bag first."

Hall went along and this time it did not occur to me to protest. As he had said, he had a stake in this game himself. I could have sworn that I saw the man with graying hair standing on the curb when we came out of the Beekman Towers.

I pulled at Hall's sleeve. "That's him."

"That is he," he told me loftily. "Where was you brung up?"

"I'm serious, Hall."

"I know you are."

"But if it is Scott?"

He had given my address to the cabbie but now he changed his mind. "Wait a minute, driver. Mattie, do you know where Hope Bancroft lives?"

"Yes, she's in that big apartment building east of Fifth Avenue on Fifty-fifth. She mentioned it the other day."

"Okay." He gave the cabbie new instructions.

"What are you going to do?"

"Call on Hope and find out whether she actually saw Scott Jameson off on a plane or whether she just gave him a ticket and hoped for the best."

And it turned out that that was what Hope had done. She was on the telephone when we knocked at the door and she stood back in surprise, to let us in. I hardly recognized her from the tailormade sort of business woman she was at the station. She wore a long housecoat of crimson satin that molded her bust, was tight at the waist, and then billowed in wide soft folds to the floor. Her black hair was different too, softer, making her look younger and more vulnerable than her usual impersonal self.

"Martha, my dear! Hall! Make yourselves comfortable. I'll finish this call in one minute."

Actually she did it in less time than this. She said briskly, "I have some guests. Please excuse me. I'll call you later." She turned around to smile at me. She had a big living room, with a luscious couch into which you seemed to sink a foot, deep carpeting, soft chairs and subdued lighting. It was a wonderful room to rest in. And delight in. On the walls were a group of Marie Laurencins, a Monet, a Matisse, and a Van Gogh. I remembered then that her husband had been a doctor distinguished in his field.

She brushed aside my apologies for disturbing her. "I couldn't be better pleased to see anyone. How are you making out?"

So I told her about the poisoned chocolates and how Hall's opportune arrival had prevented me from eating any of them, though the thought of that brought out a cold dampness on my forehead and I surreptitiously wiped the palms of my hands on my handkerchief. Then I told her about the ransacking of Kay's rooms in search of some unknown object.

"That's funny," I broke off to say, "I haven't stopped to wonder what on earth it could be. All I'm sure of is that nothing was removed from her safe," and I told Hope about that too, about its apparently untouched contents, and the memorandum Kay had made. "There's no question in my mind that S.J. stood for Scott Jameson."

She nodded, frowning. "I think that's fairly obvious. Have you told the police?"

"Oh, yes, I told them everything."

She smiled at me. "There's something so patently honest about you, Martha, that you must have convinced them."

"You're wrong about that," I said tartly. "They think I have a persecution complex and probably sent those chocolates to myself for some obscure reason, maybe just to make myself interesting."

"Oh, nonsense."

"Well, Alan doesn't think it nonsense that someone is gunning for me."

"No, neither do I. Martha, you aren't going to stay in that apartment, are you?"

"I promised Alan I wouldn't."

She gave a little sigh of relief. "That's a sensible child. Well, you came in heavy with news. What else is there?"

"Not news," Hall said. "Questions. Or rather, one question. Did you actually see Scott Jameson get on a plane for Arizona or did you simply buy him a ticket and hope for the best?"

"Well, I — well, of course, he went. What else could he do?" She lighted a cigarette, stared at it and then broke it and dropped it into a crystal ashtray. She frowned and then automatically lifted a small hand and smoothed out the wrinkles. "I didn't see him go. We had three drinks at the airport — at least, he had three. I had only one because I had work to do in the evening, preparing some data for that insurance outfit — and he was more than half-lit. I gave him his ticket and when the plane was called I saw him staggering toward the runway. I didn't wait to see him get on, but — I can't see what you are getting at."

"Kay with an ice pick in her back," Hall said deliberately; "Mattie with a box of chocolates flavored with strychnine; Kay's rooms ransacked —"

"And today," I added, "someone has been following me."

There was an odd expression on Hope's face then, the one I had seen on the detective's face. Persecution complex, she was thinking. It's funny how hard it is to convince people when you are telling them the simple, unadorned truth. It made me think of Mark Twain's answer to the line about truth being stranger than fiction. "Of course, it is; fiction has to make sense."

"Let me know the number of his flight and I'll check up," Hall said suddenly.

"You'll have to ask Hazel, my secretary. She bought the ticket. I simply can't remember. I'll let you know in the morning."

"What does he look like?" I asked suddenly.

"Scott? Why — there's nothing special about him. Nearly Alan's age, forty, and much the same type except that he's gone to seed and doesn't take care of himself so he looks older. Graying hair, his face rather lined."

When we rose to go, Hope asked, "Will you be all right tomorrow, Martha? I mean — I can't go to the service, you know. I'll have to handle things at the station."

"Of course. I'm going with Alan."

She turned to Hall. "I'm so glad Martha has you to help her at a time like this. Terribly sorry to hear you aren't planning to do another play for us. I suppose you know, if you should change your mind, or the money runs out, we'll welcome you back with open arms. There are at least three sponsors champing at the bit for a chance to back your shows because they are prestige items."

"Thank you, ma'am." He gave her a mock bow.

Hope looked from one to the other, her face troubled. Then she said, more directly and tactlessly than was customary for her, "You are going to a hotel, aren't you, Martha?"

Hall laughed. "Nothing improper is going to happen to Mattie tonight."

"Well —" She let it go.

From Hope's apartment we walked back to mine. Hall took my key, unlocked the door, and went in first, turning on lights, looking around before he grinned and said, "Pass, friend, all is well." He checked me on my way to retrieve a suitcase. "Mattie, I've got a kind of idea. Don't start yelling bloody murder until I've spoken my piece."

"I don't yell bloody murder," I said indignantly.

"You might." Hall pushed me into my favorite chair and settled himself in the lounge chair as if he belonged there. "About this hotel business, I have a kind of hunch. Someone searched Kay's house looking for something. It's quite possible that someone wants to search this apartment, looking for the same thing. That memorandum of Kay's means she intended to tell you something or give you something."

"But she didn't."

"Someone does not know that."

"Well?"

"So tonight I am going to camp out here and have a word with this person when or if he appears."

"No!" I exclaimed.

"Bloody murder," he said softly.

"No," I said more quietly. "Why should you take a risk like that? Let's call the police and have them stake out the apartment."

"And warn off the intruder? Nonsense. No, Mattie, please listen. Until we've nailed this guy down, he is going to be bad medicine; he's going to keep you awake nights — or put you to sleep permanently. Better clear it up once and for all."

"And what if he is violent?"

"That," Hall said, "is where I will surprise you. Unforbidding as I appear I am a mighty man. I have studied judo and karate and if I can get close enough —"

"And if he has a gun —"

"Spoilsport."

"Well, there's one thing sure. You aren't going to stay here and face any intruder by yourself. If you stay I stay."

"You will do nothing of the kind."

But I won that round — or I thought at the time I did. I made up the couch for Hall while he mixed himself a nightcap from the considerably lowered contents of the bottle of Scotch he had brought me. Then when I started to close my bedroom door he said, "Oh, no, you don't. Tonight you sleep on the couch and I'll take your room."

"But —"

"There's a chain on the door," he explained patiently, "and the windows are barred. No one can get in here. But there are no bars on the back windows, probably a fire law or something. I'm taking that room." He stopped my protest by the simple expedient of kissing me. He released me rather quickly. "Don't start anything you can't finish, Canfield," he said, and went into the bedroom, closing the door in my face.

Ten

The couch might as well have been a bed of nails for all the rest I got. I turned and twisted, pulled up blankets and pushed them down again. I was too hot and too cold. I remembered Alan tossing sleepless on this couch and my eyes stung with tears for him, Alan who, even in the midst of his grief and shock, had time to worry about my welfare. I tried to put away all thought of him. There was something indecent about thinking of him tonight while tomorrow Kay's lovely body would be consumed by fire.

I dredged up every living memory I had of Kay, for so many years a remote and glamorous figure whom I barely knew and rarely saw because of the difference in our ages. Always, even when she was a girl, people had been aware of her wherever she went. She engendered a kind of excitement, quite apart from her good looks, that made anything she did a happening. She had an almost greedy zest for life. I was glad now that, as her time was to be cut so short, she had lived it to the full.

I thought of all her generosity to me. She had clothed me and housed me and given me that winter at an art school in Boston. She had been at least a little fond of me, and she had trusted me. "The only human I have ever completely trusted."

And that brought me to the safe and to that memorandum about Scott Jameson. But why, I wondered, had she failed to tell me what she had discovered the time I saw her at the Plaza? All she had said was that she counted on me to stand by her when the time came, so she must have meant to tell me eventually. And someone must think that she had told me. Otherwise the poisoned candy was pointless.

So that brought me to Scott Jameson. It was obvious now, though he would not commit himself, that Lieutenant Saunders did not believe in the mugging. It was unlikely he believed in Scott Jameson either, at least as a threat to Kay. What he thought about the chocolates I did not know, but I had a terrifying suspicion he thought I had rigged them myself as a red herring because I had had a hand in Kay's death. At least they could not believe I had killed her myself as I had been at the switchboard all that day except from twelve to one when I had gone out for lunch, and she had been alive at that time, alive and — incredibly — in my apartment.

I sat up and shook my pillow and turned it over. This time I was going to lie perfectly still. Tossing and turning only kept me awake. In about one minute I was curled up in a knot.

I kept thinking of the man with the graying hair who had appeared outside Kay's house and reappeared outside the police station and Beekman Towers. Scott had graying hair, Hope had said.

Under the bedroom door seeped the smell of cigarette smoke. So Hall wasn't sleeping either. It occurred to me that Alan, if he knew, would feel that I had not kept my promise to him, but all I had promised was not to stay in the apartment alone. His comment about wolves disturbed me. There was nothing of the wolf about Hall that I could see. His interest was less in me than in finding out who had been making use of his name, who wanted to get into the apartment.

I remembered Hope's troubled expression when she had seen Hall with me. Certainly she had the highest respect for his work. She had assured him that he'd be welcomed back with open arms "when the money runs out." There seemed to be a lot

159

of talk about Hall's money. And she had been fairly straightforward in her anxiety about Hall's intentions for the night.

That brought me to Hall's insistence on staying here, in case anyone came. If I was following his reasoning, someone had sent the poisoned chocolates to eliminate me, but that would not have made it easier to get into the apartment and search for something Kay might have left there. If I had been poisoned the place would, I felt fairly sure, have been sealed off while an investigation was being made. No, the only explanation for the chocolates was someone's determination to silence me forever.

I turned over on my face, hearing muted sounds of traffic, footsteps echoing on the pavement just outside the window, the throb of an airplane overhead. There were shots from the apartment above where my neighbor was watching a late show on television, which brought me back to the days when Alan and his friend Scott had acted in western movies.

I turned on my side, my knees drawn up, and thought about Hall and what his real attitude toward Kay had been. According to Hope he had never forgiven Alan for snatching her away from under his nose. But Hall had spoken as though his interest in her had

160

been at a much earlier period and he had not only recovered from it but he did not even like her very much.

I tried to remember his alibi for the time of Kay's death. He had lunched alone, he had worked at the public library, he had dined alone in a big restaurant where he was unlikely to be noticed. An alibi that was no alibi.

But why would Hall have sent me the chocolates and used his own name? Why? And he had been determined to spend the night in this apartment, a determination that had no amorous overtones.

I could not stay in bed any longer. I got up and, without turning on the light, groped for my clothes and got dressed. Then I stretched out in the lounge chair. I felt better prepared to face anything that might happen. What happened is that, once I had stretched out and turned my cheek against the cool surface of the upholstery, I fell asleep.

It was Hall's yell that awakened me and I was standing beside the chair, clinging to its back, almost before I was aware that I was awake.

I saw the crack of light under his door, heard a crash as he moved, and a curse. I switched on the lamp beside the chair then and ran to the door.

"Hall," I called frantically, "what is it? Are you all right?"

After a moment he opened the door to me. He had not undressed; he still wore his trousers and an undervest but no shoes. He hobbled over to the bed and sat down. A glance at the overturned bedside table told its own story. He had fallen over it in the dark and stubbed his toe. I knew just how painful this can be but it was an ignominious ending to an act of derring-do and I was put to it not to giggle.

He evidently saw the amusement in my face and he smiled sourly. "Okay, kid, have your fun. I don't begrudge it."

"What happened?"

"I let him get away," he said in disgust, and that wiped the laughter out of me more effectively than anything else could have done.

"You mean he — someone — actually broke in!"

He pointed to the window which stood wide open on the dark court. As I started toward it he shook his head. "No one there now. By the time I'd got disentangled from that thrice accursed table he was out of the window and running like hell across the court."

"But where did he go?"

"Out through the service entrance of that building across the court. He didn't try to go up the stairs here because that would have taken him out in front where the street is brightly lighted."

Car doors slammed and feet pounded down the basement stairs. I lunged toward Hall and gripped his arm, while we stared at each other in a wild surmise.

Then there was a pounding on the door. "I'll answer," Hall said chivalrously, thrust me behind him, and went to open the door on the chain. "Who's there?"

"Police. Open up."

Hall took off the chain and flung open the door. The two men from the prowl car were both young enough still to feel rather tense at encountering an unknown danger. Each had his revolver in his hand.

"Welcome," Hall said with a flourish. "Sorry, but you're too late for the party."

"What party?"

"Housebreaker. He came in through the bedroom window and when I started for him I fell over the bedside table and stubbed my toe." He grinned ruefully. "Very funny, of course. But it gave the guy a chance to get away."

The policeman looked around the room

and noticed that I was fully dressed and that Hall was nearly clothed. "Looks like you were expecting this party."

"Well, we didn't send out any invitations but there seemed to be a good chance. That, by the way, is why I am here."

"Whose apartment is this?"

"It's mine," I intervened. "I am Martha Pelham. This is —"

"Let him speak for himself, lady."

Hall grinned at me. "An excellent idea. Make a note of it for future reference. I am Hall Canfield. The reason I am here is that Miss Pelham had an unpleasant experience this morning and it seemed like a good idea to keep an eye on her."

He told the two men about the box of poisoned chocolates which had been sent to me in his name and how he had fortunately just happened to call on me before I had a chance to eat one. All this was perfectly true, of course, but every time I heard it the thing seemed to sound more unlikely. Particularly that bit about Hall "just happening" to call immediately after I received the candy.

"Have you reported this to the police?" one of the men asked skeptically.

"Oh, yes, of course." Hall described the steps he had taken, the analysis of the poison by a pharmacist, and the report to the police. The mention of strychnine wiped the smiles off their faces.

One of the men, with a muttered word to his companion, went out to the police car where I assumed he was checking with the police station on our story.

"Did you get a load of the man who broke in?" the other policeman asked Hall.

He shook his head. "The light in here was out, of course and there's only a dim glow in the court where they seem to have about a forty-watt bulb. So he was just a moving shadow. If it hadn't been for that damned table I'd have caught him."

"But you were pretty sure something was scheduled to happen to Miss Pelham."

"I thought it more than likely," Hall told him grimly. "Her half-sister was Mrs. Alan Lambert, the former Kay Spaulding, who died on Thursday with a couple of icepick stabs in her back."

"Oh! I remember the case. A mugging."

"That's not what I think. It's not what the police think, either, though they aren't unburdening themselves to me."

The policeman grinned. "Well, they don't, as a rule."

He could see Hall's tumbled bed from where we sat as well as my unmade couch.

One thing he was unlikely to suspect was any kind of dalliance. He asked for Hall's address and his occupation and then took down mine as well.

"If you were so worried about Miss Pelham's safety, Mr. Canfield, why didn't you tell the police? That's what we're here for."

"We gave them the chocolates. We told them everything we knew."

"They don't believe I'm in danger," I said. "I think they believe I fixed those chocolates myself to make myself interesting or something. And they didn't believe me about the man who is following me."

By now the other policeman had returned and nodded briefly to his companion. They exchanged a speaking look.

"That's what I mean," I said hotly. "You don't really believe me! But if Hall hadn't been here —"

"That's right," one of the men said. They got up to leave. "Mr. Canfield was right on hand to protect you, wasn't he? Too bad he never caught sight of the intruder. Good night."

"Hey!" It was Hall who spoke. I was too angry to get out a word. It would have been obvious to a child that they believed Hall had staged the whole thing to make time with me, that there had never been an intruder. It was Hall who either did not notice their attitude or chose to ignore it. "Hey, just a minute there. Who told you to come here?"

"Woman upstairs. Called the police. She said it wasn't any business of hers how many men you had spending the nights here but she wasn't going to put up with all the yelling that was going on."

"I yelled only once," Hall said.

"Yeah, that's what you said. When the guy climbed out through the window."

Hall went into the bedroom, closed and locked the window, took the key out of the bedroom door, closed and locked it on the outside. He began to shrug into his jacket.

"Don't let us hurry you," one of the policemen said, grinning.

"I don't think he'll be back tonight." Hall was carefully holding on to his temper.

"Somehow I don't either."

Hall followed them out. "Keep the chain on, Mattie, but I don't think you'll be bothered again tonight, not as long as the intruder believes I am here."

"You're going?" I could not keep the chagrin and near panic out of my voice.

"I got an idea while I was lying there thinking tonight, a queer idea that we've been looking at this thing upside down.

167

Keep your chin up tomorrow, Mattie." His hand tightened on my shoulder. "I know it's going to be tough. I'd be with you but I've got to see a man — about a dog. I'll keep in touch. And tomorrow I'll get you a room at the Beekman Towers. Good night, kid." He touched my cheek with his finger and followed the two policemen up the stairs and out onto the street. I heard him say a restrained "good night" and then he walked off down the street.

Eleven

Next morning Hall called to say he had booked me a room at Beekman Towers under the name of Mary Putnam, though he had told the manager the truth about my identity so there would be no question of false registration. He had explained that it was simply a device for my own safety and the manager — Hall had lived there for five years — assured him that he would tell no one.

"I think I'm on to something, Mattie," and there was excitement in Hall's voice. "Tell you later."

The service for Kay had been scheduled for ten o'clock in the morning in the hope that the early hour would be helpful in keeping away any curious people who might get wind of it. Mansfield admitted me to Kay's house, black armband sewed neatly on his coat sleeve. With his usual kindness Alan had given him permission to attend the service.

"Miss Pelham! There's something —"

Alan came out to greet me, a gray-faced Alan who looked as though he had not slept for a week, and took me into the dining room to meet Kay's lawyer and a solemn representative from the Spaulding Company. The men were standing aimlessly around the table at which Mansfield had set out an urn of coffee and some hot rolls. Men are always more at a loss than women at a funeral and they moved restlessly and self-consciously around the room, looking at pictures, finding nothing to say.

When I refused coffee and rolls Alan took me into Kay's little room, looking out on the garden, dismal now under a chilly spring rain that fell slanting on the stunted tree in its tub and the crocuses, purple and yellow, which were scattered through the place, their fragile blossoms beaten down by the rain.

"Hotel all right?" he asked.

"I didn't go to one, after all."

"But you promised me not to stay alone. It might not be safe, Martha."

"I wasn't alone. Hall stayed."

"Hall!" Alan searched my face anxiously. "What's going on between you two, Martha? Hall is not the man for you. You can't be serious about him."

"It's not the way you think, Alan. Hall is angry because someone sent those poisoned chocolates and used his name, and he thought if there was any chance of the man trying to get at me again he wanted to catch him."

"But no one came, of course."

"Someone came, but Hall scared him away. And the woman upstairs heard the uproar and called the police. They didn't believe us. They thought Hall was just trying to make me see him as a hero by staging the whole thing."

"And do you see him as a hero?" he asked gravely.

"Oh, of course not!"

"Martha." Alan's voice broke. "Good God! Take care of yourself, darling." It was as though the words had been wrenched out of him and I found myself breathless, my heart tumbling just anyhow. As though aware of his self-betrayal, he said hastily, "Martha, I want you to have something of Kay's as a memento. A piece of her jewelry, perhaps."

"Oh, no, Alan. Honestly, I'd rather not."

Seeing that I meant it he looked around helplessly and then saw the matched set of airplane luggage standing beside her pretty desk. "She ordered this set and it's just been delivered and it doesn't have her initials yet. Take it, won't you, please?"

When I agreed, rather for his satisfaction

than my own, for the chances of needing four pieces of airplane luggage were too remote to contemplate, he nodded. "Good. I'll have them delivered to your apartment right away."

He took me back to the dining room and glanced at his watch. "If you are ready, gentlemen."

We got into Kay's big Lincoln, with Mansfield sitting in front with the chauffeur.

The man from the Spaulding Company was large and portly, good-looking, well-dressed, like any American president between 1870 and 1900, without the whiskers. But it was he, who seemed too self-possessed to display any personal feelings, who ejaculated in shocked protest, "Jesus!" as the chauffeur with some difficulty maneuvered the car in at the curb in front of the funeral parlor.

There were four policemen trying to hold back the disorderly crowd, which surged forward to look at us more closely. Flashlight bulbs exploded, cameras clicked, and reporters broke through the lines. As the mob closed in, Alan, rigid and ghastly, put his arm around me and forced his way through the crowd, protecting me as well as he could, and even so, someone pulled at me so hard that a button broke off my coat.

"Mr. Lambert, you willing to wait until you're sixty to collect on the Spaulding estate? . . . Hey, look this way, Lambert? Have you any theory about your wife's murder?"

A woman said clearly, "I don't know who the girl is. Real pretty, though. But he's just as attractive as he looks on TV, isn't he? Not handsome, of course, but he's got something. That's for sure."

One woman actually plucked at his arm and thrust an autograph album into his hand.

Again it was the man from Spaulding's who knocked it aside, snarling, "Good God, have you no decency, woman?" and he helped force a path for Alan and me through the mob.

Inside, a couple of policemen flung their weight against the doors to close them, shutting out the staring, mindless mob, leaving us in a dim room where an organ throbbed softly and the air was thick with the scent of roses, white roses, and a great spray of yellow rosebuds. I remembered that Hall had sent me yellow roses and wondered if they were his gift. My violets, at my request, had been placed in Kay's hand.

There was some uneasy rustling and the men stirred in their chairs. One of them automatically reached for his cigarette case and then, in embarrassment, thrust it out of sight. One of the policemen guarding the doors coughed and tried to stifle the sound. And then the music stopped and Kay's minister began to speak quietly. He had known her all her stormy life, he had refused to perform her last two marriage services because he did not recognize divorce, but now he recalled her great zest for life, the candle that had burned so fiercely and so rapidly, spoke of her with love and of her death with compassion.

Then the organ began to play again and the coffin sank into the floor. I clutched Alan's arm, looked into his rocklike face, and stumbled to my feet.

One of the attendants who had stood in grave and respectful silence during the brief service stopped me rather hastily as I went down the room toward the door.

"There's quite a mob outside there, miss. Mr. Jenkins suggests you go out by the door to the service alley. Your car will pick you up on Madison in the next block."

He led the way and we trooped out, Alan supporting me, as I was shaking so badly I could hardly stand. Rain was falling heavily now but it felt cool on my face.

Alan shook hands briefly with the men

who uttered some banal words of sympathy and went away in haste, not altogether because of the rain, but escaping from that dark funeral parlor and the scent of roses, and the ghouls who waited in front to stare at people who had been bereaved in a peculiarly horrible way, to escape back to the reassuring bustle and problems of the living.

"Don't take me home," I said. "I'm going to walk."

"But it's raining."

"I don't mind rain. I've got to walk, Alan."

"Are you going back to the apartment?"

"Just to pack a bag. I promised Hall I'd go to a hotel until — this is all over."

"Hall? Oh, yes, of course. All right, dear. But be careful, won't you? Nothing must happen to you."

"It won't."

Mansfield, who had been standing beside the Lincoln, looking old and shaken, said, "Miss Pelham, may I offer you my sympathy?"

"Not now, Mansfield," Alan intervened. "Miss Pelham has had about all she can take this morning."

I nodded to the old man and started walking down the street, unaware of people unless I bumped into them, unaware of traffic lights until a policeman jerked me back onto the sidewalk practically from under the wheels of a taxi, and said, "Can't you read, lady? It says, 'Don't walk'?"

I mumbled, "Sorry," and stopped to lean against a store front and get myself under control before I went on bumbling into people like one of those great swollen houseflies. The window was that of an art gallery and the picture it displayed was a French Impressionist. I remembered Hope's beautiful paintings and longed to be able to talk to her. Maybe in her comforting presence I could drive away the horror that was making me sick. But Hope, of course, was at the station, making sure that Alan's spot was filled, and arranging for someone to take over my job. Hope who never failed.

And then I went on in the rain again.

When I got back to the apartment I was chilled and soaked through. The superintendent, who had been struggling with a recalcitrant hot-water heater, came to the door carrying the matched luggage. "This was just delivered for you."

I stripped and took a hot shower, standing under it until the coldness had left my body and the needle spray had sent the warm blood coursing through my veins. I rubbed my hair dry, thanking heaven not for the first time that it had a natural wave, put on blue jeans and a red blouse, rolled up my sleeves, and got to work to clean the apartment. I swept and polished and dusted, stripped the beds and put my laundry together, and, when the place was in apple-pie order, I went out to a laundromat where, mercifully, no one recognized me.

When I came back with my bundle of clean clothes I was hungry at last. I fixed some breakfast and felt the better for it. I had just cleaned up the dishes when there was a tap at the door.

It was the woman from upstairs. I had never seen her so close before. She was about forty, medium height and rather overweight, wearing a dingy brown dress with fringe like a hippie, and dangling earrings that must have come from the five and ten. She held a letter in her hand.

She looked at me, at the jeans and the red shirt, and said, "I thought it was only right to warn you that I've written a letter to the realty company asking them to put you out as an undesirable tenant."

She edged past me, determined to see all there was to be seen. "Well, I must say, you keep this place real nice. I wouldn't have thought you could do so much to a basement." She was around me now and she stepped into the living room. "It's not my business how you want to live. I didn't call the police last night just because you had a man staying here, but when it comes to shouting in the middle of the night —"

"There was a housebreaker and the man who stayed to look after me shouted and fell over a table in the dark so the man got away. I suppose you didn't catch sight of him."

Her eyes widened. "You mean there was a burglar? Well, there! No," she added regretfully, "I didn't see anyone. Just heard that yell. But I've been worried; once a girl starts letting men stay that way, she is headed for trouble. I saw that Alan Lambert, the TV man, leave here the other morning."

"He's my brother-in-law." As she looked incredulous I said, "His wife, my half-sister, was murdered. He couldn't stay home, what with all the reporters and everything, and this morning we went to her service — and it was supposed to be private — and, oh God! the ghouls. There were mobs, staring, pushing, even asking Alan for his autograph, and pulling me so hard they tore a button off my coat."

And then, most improbably, I was wailing all my grief onto the breast of my neighbor and she was patting my shoulder and saying soothing, meaningless things like, "There, there."

And after a time she put the letter down on the table with a half-apologetic smile, and went away, saying at the door, "If you want me, I'm just upstairs and I'm home most of the time. My husband allows me enough alimony so I don't have to work any more. I was a beautician." She nodded and went out, closing the door softly.

When she had gone I wondered what I had been about to do when she interrupted me, wandered into the bedroom, and saw Kay's beautiful new pieces of matching airplane luggage, the smallest one an exquisitely fitted week-end bag.

I chose the next largest one, packed night things and cosmetics, hose and slips and enough dresses for the rest of the week at the station. I fastened the case and took my topcoat, now nearly dry, off its hanger, reminding myself to find a matching button. I was about to put away the other cases when there was a knock at the door, the heavy, authoritative knock I had come to recognize, and always with a sinking heart, and I admitted Lieutenant Wilkins and the heavyset man called Fischer.

"Going somewhere?" He caught sight of the suitcase. "You aren't thinking of leaving town, are you?"

"I'm going to a hotel. I promised my

brother-in-law I wouldn't stay here any longer." I told him about the housebreaker of the night before and I could see he already knew the story. So far as I could make out he didn't believe it. Not by anything he said, for he never said much, but by a kind of tightening of his face.

"You'd better sit down," I told him, because I realized I couldn't stand much longer.

His eyes sharpened. "You all right, Miss Pelham?"

"My sister was — they held the service for her this morning. It was unspeakable! Those ghouls! Those horrible ghouls. Staring and pointing and trying to crowd in, to see anything there was to see."

"Yes," he said abruptly, "I got a report. Sometimes you wonder if people are worth all the trouble we take and the risks we run to keep them safe."

"I didn't know people could act like that."

"People," he said somberly, "are capable of anything. You learn that in my job. All the way from a kind of heroism you wouldn't believe possible, often just ordinary guys risking their lives for total strangers. And all the way to the unspeakable, to behavior that would disgust an animal. Well," as though ashamed of this uncharacteristic burst of feeling, "let's get on with it." He went over the housebreaking, Hall's presence, and the intruder's escape. He nodded noncommittally. I told him that I was pretty sure I had seen the graying man in the crowd at the funeral, and he nodded at that too.

"You just don't believe me, do you?" I said despairingly.

"We want to get at the truth, Miss Pelham. We won't overlook anything."

"Why are you convinced that Kay was murdered not by a chance mugger but because she was Kay?"

He hesitated. "I don't see why I shouldn't tell you," he said after due deliberation, and I saw Fischer look at him in surprise. "Please understand, Miss Pelham, we have not come to a definite conclusion that it was that kind of murder. It might still be just another mugging with the victim chosen at random. But when a woman as sensationally wealthy as Kay Spaulding — I mean Mrs. Lambert — dies by violence, there are bound to be questions, because there is a hell of a lot — excuse me — at stake. And in this case, your sister was notor— famous for her reckless exploits. She was, to put it bluntly, the kind of woman who makes enemies, the kind to whom things happen."

Hall had made the same remark. Hall had

said I should thank God I wasn't like that.

Lieutenant Wilkins examined his fingernails thoughtfully, turning his hand this way and that. "Then there were other things. There was that valuable wristwatch with its diamond-studded bracelet, which was left behind. Now there's only one reasonable explanation we can see for abandoning a thing like that. It had stopped at two o'clock, so it might be intended to provide a useful alibi for someone."

"But I thought an autopsy would establish the time of death."

"There were certain factors that confused the issue, and made it more difficult. For instance, she had eaten no lunch."

"She never did. She was reducing, though she didn't need to."

"Then it turned cold that night. And, of course, as time goes on the difficulty in establishing the exact moment of death is proportionately increased." He looked at me to see whether I understood this. "Actually the death might have occurred any time between twelve-thirty and six-thirty."

"But the superintendent says she was here at twelve-thirty, here at my apartment, for five minutes at least."

He nodded. "Well, there is the stolen car in which she was found. The only reason for moving the body to the stolen car was to postpone for as long a time as possible its discovery. In the case of a routine mugging this would have served no purpose."

"How do you know she was moved, Lieutenant? Perhaps there was some reason for her getting voluntarily into the car; for instance, to speak to someone she knew. Like those people she mentioned when she called home and talked to Mansfield."

"We know she was moved because her jacket was saturated with her blood and there were only a few faint smears on the car upholstery. The car was driven into the parking building at four-thirty and left in an obscure corner on the top floor. That's the time of the day when most cars are moving in and out and there was no particular reason for noticing it. And it was one of those buildings where the driver takes a ticket, with the time stamped, from a machine, so no one was on hand to look at the occupants of the car."

"So there's nothing at all to go on?"

"Somewhere," Wilkins told me, "there's a lot of evidence I'd give my eyeteeth to get my hands on. Take all that blood — and it must have spurted — and the ammonia spray, which had been emptied. The evidence is somewhere. It's harder than you may realize to get rid of clothes that have stains of such a nature and not leave some clue to their ownership." He asked abruptly, "When, where, and with whom did you lunch the day Mrs. Lambert was killed?"

I was so angry that it was a moment before I could speak quietly. "I always lunch from twelve to one and I ate that day, as I always do, alone, as I don't know many of the people at the station very well yet. I got a sandwich at a drugstore counter because I found a run in my pantihose and I had to go shopping before I went back to work." I stared at him. "But, Lieutenant, no woman could possibly have killed Kay. Why a woman could not have lifted her into a car. She was no featherweight. And I was at the station all afternoon. You can ask anyone."

"Let me see. Mr. Canfield was working at the library all afternoon, I believe, and Mr. Lambert, after doing his usual show, made a speech at a reception for Mr. Cosgrave."

"Alan! But you can't believe — and Hall! Why in heaven's name would Hall want to hurt Kay?"

"I don't believe anything, miss. I'm just checking. And checking. And re-checking. But we've talked to half a dozen people who saw Mr. Lambert at the reception and remember him making the speech and saw him circulating among the guests, pretty well the whole time. And if he had taken part in the murder of his wife he could not have escaped having his coat badly stained. And no one noticed any change in his clothing, certainly no staining of any kind was visible."

"So?" I said challengingly.

"Of course, Mr. Canfield's alibi is much more difficult to check. Practically impossible unless we make public what we're looking for and someone comes forward who happened to see him at the crucial times. Things like that occur, of course, but not very often. People don't want to get involved and, in a way, you can't blame them. For a businessman it might mean having to hold himself available to testify in court. And there are people who might find difficulty in explaining satisfactorily just why they happened to be in New York and in the parking building at that time. And then some people just naturally run for cover."

"You don't have a high opinion of the human race, Lieutenant."

"No, I haven't." To my surprise he smiled. "But it's the best we've been able to produce up to now so I guess we'd better accept it."

He sounded so nearly human that I found myself smiling back, a response to which he was obviously unaccustomed because he became impersonal and professional again.

"But there is one point on which we are pretty well agreed, Miss Pelham. Two people were involved in Mrs. Lambert's death, whether muggers or —" He let that drop.

He means Hall and me, I thought, and, ridiculous as the idea was, I felt afraid.

"Have you checked on Scott Jameson?"

"We got the flight number from Mrs. Bancroft's secretary. No one occupied his seat on that flight, if it interests you."

"At least it's plain to see that you aren't interested! I keep trying to tell you that Scott Jameson is dangerous. Hope Bancroft knows it. Kay knew something about him and look what happened to her. And someone thinks I know the same thing and someone is following me. Someone sent me poisoned candy and someone is trailing me. Someone tried to get in here last night. I'm not making this up. I've seen the man with the graying hair at least four times in the past twenty-four hours and I'm pretty sure he was at the funeral this morning! I suppose when I'm found dead you'll begin to wonder about him."

I might as well not have spoken. Lieutenant Wilkins glanced at his companion and said, "We'll be in touch. Where will you be spending the night?"

"At the Beekman Towers. Mr. Canfield arranged it for me."

"So we can reach you there if necessary."

"Well — yes." It did seem furtive when I explained it. "You see, Mr. Canfield didn't want trouble about false registration so he told the manager who I really am, but I'll be registered as Mary Putnam. Just to avoid people like those — those ghouls —" and again I began to shake.

Fischer made a note of the name and the two men went away. To check. And check. And re-check.

I made a last inspection of the apartment, tested the lock on the bedroom window, and picked up Kay's suitcase. When I went out on the street I saw a man turn in at the little French bakery. For a moment it seemed to me that there was the familiar thatch of graying hair but at this point I felt fatalistic. No one cared. Go ahead and do your worst, I apostrophized the man silently and walked away without a second look. The rain had stopped and a watery kind of sunshine filtered down into the narrow canyons of the streets.

In the lobby of Beekman Towers a bellhop seized my suitcase and led me to the desk, where I said, speaking as naturally as I could but feeling horribly self-conscious, I think a room has been reserved for me for the remainder of the week. Mary Putnam."

The desk clerk looked up without interest and reached for a card which he pushed forward for me to sign and took down a key.

"Oh, yes, Miss Putnam. Twelfth floor. Nice view. I hope you'll be comfortable. Glad to have you with us."

He handed the key to the waiting bellhop, actually a sharp-faced man in his middle-thirties, who took me up in the elevator, unlocked a door, switched on lights, threw up the window, indicated the bathroom, and set down the suitcase with a flourish. When I had tipped him he gave me a swift, curious look and went out.

Before dinner I went up to the cocktail lounge on the roof and ordered a Manhattan and sipped it slowly and gratefully, while I looked out at the lights of the city and remembered Kay would never see them again, she who had so loved the bright lights and the noise and the excitement. But it was sorrow I felt now as the horror was beginning to fade.

After dinner I could not face returning to that empty room. This was one time when I really needed Hall and he had not come near me or telephoned or anything. And I didn't want to be alone. I couldn't face a movie so at last I wandered down the street into a bar, where at least there would be other people. The television was blaring, showing men dying in Cambodia and, of course, Ireland, where brother continues to slaughter brother with undiminished enthusiasm, and at last, for a change, turned to crime in the United States.

"This morning Kay Spaulding, born Kathryn Pelham, later Mrs. Brookfield and still later Mrs. Wentworth, and at the time of her death, Mrs. Alan Lambert, wife of the well-known television man, was cremated at a funeral parlor in mid-Manhattan. The service, which the family had intended to be strictly private, was stormed by hundreds of people attracted by the murder of Mrs. Lambert and her husband's growing fame."

There was a mob outside the funeral parlor, with the police attempting to hold them back, and Alan, looking like death itself, with his arm around me. "The widower and his sister-in-law," the commentator said in a dry voice and my face burned. It was like being in a pillory and what he implied was not true.

And I could hear Alan, his voice breaking, say, "Take care of yourself, darling." So I paid for the untouched glass of beer and went out of the little bar into the spring night.

In my room at the Beekman I slipped on a robe and then sat in the dark looking out at the lights of Long Island until the telephone jangled shrilly and I groped for it.

"Miss Martha Pelham?"

Taken unaware, I said, "Yes. Oh, hello, Hall, I've been hoping you'd call."

There was a laugh. "That's what I thought!" The caller rang off.

I sat staring at the silent phone. Only Hall and the police knew where I was staying.

After a while I had the switchboard ring Hall's apartment. He answered promptly.

"Hall?"

"You okay, Mattie? Are you installed here?"

"Yes, except — Hall, someone just called and said, 'Miss Martha Pelham,' and I didn't think and said 'yes' and he laughed and said he thought so, and hung up."

"Hell and damnation!"

"Did you tell anyone where I was?"

"Of course not. Except the manager here and he's trustworthy. I heard about that scene this morning. What a rotten thing for you to go through. Poor Mattie!"

Then why didn't you do something about

it, you great goop! Letting me have dinner alone. Letting me come back to this frightening room alone. I swallowed my indignation and said nothing at all.

"Look here," he said, "I've been thinking and I'm pretty sure I can guess how that telephone call happened. Anyhow I can check it out right away." He added somberly, "God knows I never meant you to be involved in all this, Mattie, but you'll be all right. I've got to go now. I've got to see a man, a couple of men."

"But, Hall —"

I heard him break the connection.

Twelve

I awoke in the strange hotel room the next morning, heavy-eyed from a restless night. After my dark basement the lights had kept me awake: the lights, and the memory of that obscene mob outside the funeral parlor, and Wilkins's flat voice saying that two people had been involved in the murder, that all our alibis were being checked.

That morning the sky was blue, without a hint of smog, and the air was almost warm. I crossed the street at First Avenue and was startled when Hall, who was leaning against a post, smoking a cigarette, tossed it into the gutter and took my arm.

"Did you have any breakfast?"

"In the coffee shop. I didn't know that you ever got out at this early hour."

"I don't as a rule. I just thought it might be a sound idea to provide you with a bodyguard." He looked down at me. "Just a precaution. Now what happened? Tell papa."

Obediently I told him about Wilkins's visit and the police theory in regard to Kay's death.

"Two people? Yes, I guess it would take two."

"Hall, who on earth was responsible for that call last night?"

"I know who was responsible," he said grimly. "The bellhop. I've had suspicions about him for a long time."

"The bellhop called me?"

"No, he gets paid so much an item by a gossip columnist. He probably overheard me talking to the manager and then, when you checked in, he tipped off this guy. I taxed him with it this morning and he admitted it."

"I hope you got him fired."

Hall was apologetic. "I should have. He's such a smelly little rat. But he helps support his mother and it's hard for an untrained, unintelligent guy to get a job these days, you know. At least he's seen the error of his ways, and he knows I'll take him apart if he does it again."

As we walked toward the station I looked around but there was no sign of the man I felt sure was Scott.

At the station business was going on as usual. I took over the switchboard, thinking how odd it was that everything had changed and yet nothing had changed. I had dreaded having to cope with curiosity from station people but they asked no questions and, beyond a few words of sympathy, they let me alone.

Hope came in, smiled, and kissed me lightly on the cheek. "Why don't you come home with me tonight? I should have thought of it before but there has been a lot on my so-called mind. I have an extra bedroom and you can stay as long as you like."

I explained that Hall had arranged for me to have a room at Beekman Towers and she looked at me, half perplexed, half amused.

"No one would believe you and Kay are sisters. You're the most," she groped for a word, "unsophisticated girl of your age I've ever encountered. Hall's a brilliant man in his own field but — oh, hell, it doesn't concern me but I'm fond of you. Do come home with me."

"Thanks a lot, Hope, but I'd rather stay put."

"I suppose you know what you're doing," she said in a tone that implied she didn't suppose anything of the sort. "Well, have it your own way. You're one of those hidebound people who can't be indebted to anyone. Stiff-necked. That's what you are, my child." She was determinedly keeping everything as light as possible. "Just the same, this intransigent independence may

194

lead you into unforeseen difficulties."

"I may be unsophisticated but I'm not a complete fool, Hope. I'm in no danger from Hall. He's pulling his own chestnuts out of the fire and he's not concerned with me."

"Well, at least that's a new approach." Before she could go on someone came to ask her about an emergency and she went off quickly, with a little wave of the hand and a rueful shake of the head.

A few minutes later the girl who played Angela came in with her usual harassed rush. She stopped short when she saw me.

"I'm terribly sorry, Martha. Just terribly sorry. I didn't even know until yesterday that you were related to her. Everyone wants to tell you how they feel but they don't want to get in your hair."

I nodded. After all, there was nothing to be said.

"Hope here?"

"She came in just a few minutes ago."

"Is she free?"

"Is she ever? Apparently something has come unstuck and she is handling it."

"Dear Hope! What would we do without her? She took me in once for a whole week when I'd had to run out on my husband. He was gunning for me and Hope helped to keep me from cracking up. And now I need her help to keep the story of my divorce out of the papers. If anyone gets hold of that it would be enough to ruin me. I'm the girl who makes everything come out all right for everybody. I can't afford to spoil my image." She laughed without amusement. "So when people find I'm divorcing an alcoholic I'll be sunk. I suppose my fat-headed public would expect me to cure him with a few soft and infinitely wise words. Yah! Well, Hope will figure a way of keeping my stage name out of the news, if only to protect the interests of the station. That gal has guts."

I looked at her, wan and drawn with emotional strain, her marriage to a man she once must have loved breaking up after what must have been a number of ugly scenes and the humiliation and degradation attendant on alcoholism, but she was prepared to carry on with her taxing job as usual.

"I think you have more guts than any of them," I told her.

Just then the door opened and Alan came in. The girl who played Angela said, "That's the one with guts. Like a rock, that man." She drifted away and Alan gave me a questioning look. Apparently I had begun to think like television people because my first impression was that the make-up man would have difficulty in covering the signs of sleeplessness. He was haggard.

"All right, Martha?"

"All right, Alan."

"No more trouble?"

I started to tell him about the anonymous telephone call the night before but it occurred to me he had enough to bear. "No more trouble. You're early, aren't you?"

"I want to see the tape of that program Hope put on in my spot yesterday and catch up with my mail, and check on the guests for the rest of the week. Some of them may need coaching and I've got to read up on the others so I'll know what questions to feed them."

"I wish you didn't have to bother."

"Thank God for something to do! I'd go crazy sitting around that house any longer."

"Can't you go away, Alan? Just for a little while? The station would understand in the circumstances. After all, if you were ill, if you had a breakdown, you'd have to take a leave of absence or something."

He stood frowning down at me, hands in his pockets. "Know what I'd really like? To be on a horse, riding across the desert, with not a human being in sight. Just the rough earth and cactus and, now and then, a road-runner, and some saguaros in the middle distance and stark hills for a background." He laughed at himself. "I'd even settle for a couple of snakes." He waved his hand and went off to work.

Alan's reference to riding in the desert made me think of Scott, and I wondered where he was now and what he was doing. If he had had a hand in Kay's death, who had assisted him? Who?

A few hours later I realized that Scott was out of the running. He might not have used the ticket Hope had bought for him but he was in Arizona. A hundred-dollar travelers' check had been cashed at Phoenix banks the day before, endorsed by Scott Jameson.

This information was given me by Lieutenant Saunders, who was waiting when I came back from lunch. On impulse I had asked Angela to go with me during her break between rehearsal and performance. She had accepted in some surprise but with pleasure and we didn't discuss our problems, hers or mine, at all. We didn't talk about television. We talked about spring and about where we had gone to school and what we usually ate for breakfast. All the important things. We both felt better when we got back to work.

At least I felt better until I caught sight of Lieutenant Saunders, who was accompanied this time by a detective named School or Schole or something like that who did nothing but sit nibbling his fingernails while Saunders did all the talking, which, of course, suited Saunders to a T.

It was only when he was leaving that the Lieutenant tossed the bombshell about Scott Jameson. What he had come to see me about was something quite different. The night before, the window in my bedroom had been jimmied open and the apartment had been ransacked.

"We're replacing the window and we've arranged to have bars put on it. From now on you'll be safe there, though it's just as well you were away last night."

"Locking the barn door," I suggested, not very politely. "If the police had believed me in the first place, or Mr. Canfield."

"Mr. Canfield," he said, with what at the moment I took to be irrelevance, "spent almost the whole night with a friend on East End Avenue. He didn't get home until nearly five. The trouble at your apartment occurred about midnight."

So we were all under surveillance.

Saunders waited patiently while I answered calls and referred incoming people to the right departments, but always, when I was free for a moment, he was back on the job.

"One thing is obvious, Miss Pelham.

Someone is hell bent on finding something. Mrs. Lambert's rooms were searched. Your rooms have been searched. *What is it?*"

"I've racked my brains trying to think. All I'm sure of, judging by the places where they have looked, is that it must be something very small."

"Are you positive that Mrs. Lambert did not tell you something you are holding back?"

"Yes, I am."

"And she left nothing with you? Nothing at all?"

"Nothing at all. The only thing in the apartment was her handkerchief and I gave you that."

He stared at me as though trying to see into my brain. "If you are holding anything back from the police you are making the mistake of your life."

"I'm not. If I knew anything I'd tell you like a shot. The only human being I can think of who would try to hurt Kay is Scott Jameson. But I've told you that over and over."

That was when he told me that Scott Jameson was in Arizona. The lieutenant left me then, but he went, I felt sure, still believing that I was withholding valuable information.

That afternoon Alan had three guests on his program, which was always a help in case one should dry up. One of them was a businessman forced into retirement by age who had created a new job for himself; one who had retired at the earliest possible moment and was discovering every day new delights in leisure; the third was a professional writer who had never contemplated any other way of life. It was fascinating to see the way Alan played them against each other, the three theories of the good life, and brought out the men's honest thinking and their real values. No one listening to him — for once I had the sound turned on low — would have believed that he had anything on his mind but a pleasant and relaxed conversation with pleasant and, fortunately, articulate people.

Hall appeared in mid-afternoon. "I wanted you to lunch with me but by the time I got back here you were gone." He sounded aggrieved, apparently under the impression that I should have awaited his pleasure and his own good time.

"I have from twelve to one and today Angela and I lunched together."

"I hope she was giving you good advice about your love life."

"She's in a lot of trouble, Hall."

"Well, don't get mixed up in it, Mattie! It's one thing to have a kind heart but you — keep — out."

"Yes, master."

"Sorry. I didn't mean to lay down the law."

"You sounded as though that was just what you did mean." It occurred to me that we were spatting like a couple of children.

"I can't take you to dinner tonight," he said, frowning. "My last play goes on at nine and I'll have to be on hand. Anyhow, my sponsor is sore as hell about my dropping out of television and I'll ply him with food and liquor to soothe his ruffled feathers. And later — uh — I've got people to see. You'll stay in your room, won't you?"

"You bet I will." I told him about the apartment having been broken into.

His mouth, usually pleasant, was ugly. "Mattie, for God's sake, *what did Kay give you?*"

I was ready to yelp with irritation and sheer frustration. "You too! For the last time, nothing at all."

He shrugged helplessly and went out, his shabby briefcase slapping against his leg. I remembered too late that I had not told him about Scott Jameson.

Alan appeared, wiping his forehead with

his handkerchief, getting rid of a trace of cold cream left by the make-up man. "Hope tells me she has asked you to stay with her for a while. You couldn't do better, Martha. I trust you'll take her up on it. At least I wouldn't have to worry about you then."

"I don't like being so beholden, Alan."

"Oh, nonsense. Hope would be delighted to have you and there's no need to feel any obligation. She lives alone, you know, and I don't suppose she likes it any better than anyone else."

"Just the same —"

"Well, what are you planning to do?"

"Hall got me a room at Beekman Towers where he lives." I added quickly, "I'm going to pay for it myself, of course. I'll stay there until the end of the week. Anyhow, I can't go back to the apartment for a few days. They have to repair the bedroom window and put on some bars."

I told him then that the apartment had been broken into and what the police planned to do about it.

He leaned over and lifted my chin with a finger. "You have a lot of trust in Hall, haven't you?"

"I — think so. Well, of course, I do. Why shouldn't I?"

"I don't know," he said heavily. "He has a

queer reputation where women are concerned, Martha. He was damned unpleasant when Kay married me, acted ugly about it, made threats. Of course, she was — lovely. But even so I do wish — oh, skip it! I just want you — to be all right. I'd ask you to have dinner with me but after that damned picture on TV, me with my arm around you — if the fools had known I was just trying to keep you from being trampled to death! Of course, in a way, it's understandable. That station has been trying to undermine me ever since I signed up where I am."

"It's all right, Alan. That doesn't matter. But I don't think we should have dinner together, in any case, while things are so upset. I can't very well go to the house and you can't go to the apartment."

"Whatever you say, dear. Only remember this: If you want me — any time — for any reason — the gossip won't matter a damn. Not a damn. Just call me and I'll be there."

"I know, Alan, and thank you."

He scanned my face, frowning. "You aren't still worried about Scott, are you?"

"No, he's in Phoenix." I explained about the travelers' check which Scott Jameson had cashed the day before.

"And that was reported to New York right

away? So the police are following up Scott in Phoenix. Poor devil! Such a good guy, Martha. You'd like him. Some day you'll get to know him and understand why I feel I can bank on him. Well, at least he is in the clear. That's the only good thing that has happened in a long time."

He turned to smile and shake hands with one of his guests whom he had arranged to have make a tour of the station.

"Glad you enjoyed it, and thank you again for being with us."

He held open the door and followed his guest out of the building without a backward glance.

Thirteen

One point was driving me crazy. If the man with graying hair who had been following me so assiduously was not Scott Jameson then who was he? There was a kind of sense in Scott trailing me if he had had a hand in Kay's murder and believed she had left me some sort of clue. There was no sense at all if he was not Scott. Try as I would I could not get the nagging questions out of my mind. Who was the man? Why was he after me?

That night I took a cab back to Beekman Towers, had dinner sent up and made the waiter identify himself before opening the door, which made him look at me oddly, though I suppose hotel employees reach a point beyond surprise at human behavior, and then locked and bolted the door and settled down to watch the television screen.

What I specially wanted to see was Hall's play, *You Can't Miss It*. It was as clever as the others and brilliantly acted by an all-star cast, and the direction was flawless: deft, swift-moving, and building to a terrific climax. Everything about it was excellent and I didn't like it; the feeling it left was one of curious discomfort; there was more sardonic wit and less compassion than in the ones that had preceded it and I was sorry that Hall was ending his current series of plays on that disillusioned note. It was like the Lunts leaving the stage after *The Visit* rather than with one of their sparkling comedies that crackled with laughter. That wasn't the way one wanted to remember them.

I switched off the program impatiently, aware that I could not expect to hear from Hall tonight. There was to be a party for him at the studio followed by a late supper at the St. Regis.

For all I saw of him, we might as well be at the ends of the earth as living in the same hotel, I thought resentfully. At any rate, Hope and Alan would have little cause to suspect his motives if they knew how little I saw of him.

I went to bed feeling abused and sorry for myself, slept soundly for nine hours, and awakened to a bright spring morning and feeling on top of the world.

After eating my first really hearty meal in days I walked to the station, not even looking back. On a bright day like this there was nothing to fear. Somehow, some way, everything was going to work out all right.

I hadn't been at my place in front of the switchboard for more than thirty minutes before I became aware that no one shared my feelings of optimism. It was one of those days when a pall hangs over everything. There had been problems on a late evening show when a comic who had appeared in high spirits, in every sense of the words, had made at least one major blunder and embarked on an off-color story, which had to be cut off, leaving everyone jittery.

A gossip snooper had got hold of the impending divorce of Angela, "the lady who provided such sound advice for the lovelorn, particularly those with marital problems," and her advertisers were up in the air about it, not wanting the taint of her divorce to injure the purity of the cereals, washing powders, and floor wax they were marketing. One of them had even suggested that it might be wise to replace her with some young woman of unblemished reputation.

Hope looked a tired and faded forty-five, her eyes strained, and her voice, for once, sharp. She was short with people who came to her with complaints.

"Can't anyone in this place do anything for himself?" she exclaimed irritably.

It was one of those days, too, when the

switchboard was never silent. Mansfield called, asked hesitantly for me, and said, "Miss Pelham, I'd like very much to see you. There's something I want to talk to you about, but not over the telephone. It wouldn't take you long and I'd feel easier in my mind. I'll come wherever you say."

"Of course, Mansfield. I'm off at five. I'll meet you — can you come to the lobby of the Beekman Towers hotel about quarter past five? That's only a short walk for you."

"Thank you very much. I'll be prompt."

After he hung up I recalled that he had tried to talk to me several times before and the idea came like a lightning flash. That is what Kay had done with her message for me, if there was a message; she had given it to Mansfield to deliver. What a fool I had been not to think of that before.

There were a number of calls for Hall from people wanting to talk to him about his play or sponsors eager to back him in a new series. I explained that Mr. Canfield was not at the station and was not expected. Any letters addressed to him at the station would be forwarded but we had no permission to give out his address.

There was also a persistent man who called half a dozen times during the morning, saying only, "Tell him it's Burt. Get in touch at once."

Alan came in just as I was leaving for lunch. He looked terrible. When I exclaimed, he managed a smile. "Headache. I can't sleep and it's getting me down. I feel as though a couple of men with hammers were hitting me on the skull."

"Well, you can't go on like this or you'll have a breakdown. You've got to see a doctor, Alan."

"Doctors can't cure this thing. If I could just know who killed Kay and why? *Why?* Maybe I could sleep again."

"Have you eaten anything?"

He looked at me blankly and then shook his head. "Some coffee."

"You can't go on like this," I repeated.

"I can damned well try."

"At least consult a doctor. Today. Promise?"

Seeing that my heart was set on it he promised, crossing his heart solemnly, winked at me, and went on.

As I emerged from the building, Hall detached himself from the trashbox against which he was leaning — that tall, lean body of his always seemed to be propped up against something — and took my arm casually as though I had been expecting him.

Though I hadn't. Not really. I'd just taken one quick look around, in case —

He signaled a cab. "Gotham."

"I only have an hour."

"We'll order something that can be served in a hurry. I just wanted to make sure you are behaving yourself."

I told him about the telephone calls, especially those from the persistent Burt. He nodded. He was in one of his most provoking moods so he didn't explain who Burt was. There were times when I could have shaken him. I was half afraid he would ask me how I'd liked his play but I should have known better. Hall didn't talk about his work and he didn't fish for compliments.

"You're looking fine today, like spring itself."

"So far it's been a horrible day. What? Oh, I haven't looked at the menu yet."

"Two club sandwiches and coffee," Hall said promptly, "and we'd appreciate it if you could hurry them. We haven't much time."

"Of course, Mr. Canfield."

I raised my brows. "You're really the big shot around here, aren't you?"

"Don't be vulgar, woman; it isn't becoming. And what's so horrible about the morning?"

"Just about everything. People seem to be

211

on edge; Hope looks tired and nervous and she's biting people's heads off. Poor Angela is in trouble because the story of her divorce leaked out, and one of her sponsors thinks she should be replaced."

"What a rotten shame! I can guess who it is, too." When Hall named him I nodded. "Okay, he belongs to one of my clubs. I'm going to tackle him, build up the poor kid and make her look like one of the heroines of her own scripts."

"You! How terribly kind."

There was a wry twist to his mouth at my involuntary surprise. "Oh, the boy has some quite nice instincts," he mocked me and I flushed with embarrassment. Damn the man! He was always putting me in the wrong. "Go on with the Lamentations."

"There's nothing really; except that Alan looks awful, Hall. He's headed for a crack-up. He's almost blind with headache and he says he can't sleep. I made him promise to see a doctor. I should think Hope would try to do something about it. After all, he's a valuable property. The station can't afford to have him break down."

"What happens to Alan matters a lot to you, doesn't it?" Hall said gently.

"Well, of course. He's my brother-in-law and —"

"Skip it." I noticed then that while I was hungrily disposing of my club sandwich he was sipping coffee and eating an olive. He eyed me somberly.

"If you think I'm involved with Alan," I began, thinking I understood the cause of his worry.

"I know you aren't." Hall was being deliberately provocative. "No, my wench, it is not the state of your maiden fancies that disturbs me."

Before I could begin a furious tirade he went on in a tone that stopped me in my tracks, "It's being borne in on me more sharply every day that I may have triggered the whole mess." He managed an unconvincing smile. "Don't sit with your mouth open like that; it makes you look like a dying carp."

"I don't think you're being very funny."

"I'm not being funny at all. I told you I thought I was on to something and the more I dig into it the more convinced I am."

"You know who killed Kay?"

He hesitated and then answered carefully as though measuring his words, "Well, at least, I think I know why. She was always shrewd, you know, in spite of that feather-headed impression she gave as though she never had a serious thought in her life. I

213

doubt if anyone could pull the wool over her eyes very long. And she was one of those people who never really trusted anyone but herself — and you."

"But what did you have to do with Kay?" There was a small cold spot in the pit of my stomach. The sandwich tasted of sawdust.

"The important thing is that I was never in love with Kay. Infatuated, yes. But only for a few weeks and that was years ago. 'That was in another country and, besides, the wench is dead.' "

"Not very good taste," I said.

"Sorry. I didn't mean to sound flippant. God knows I don't feel flippant."

"What did you mean by saying you had triggered the whole thing?"

"I'm afraid I sparked the idea that led eventually to Kay's death. You aren't hungry either?" He signaled for the waiter. "Then we'll get out of here where we can talk." He scrawled his name on the check, left a tip beside it, and followed me out of the big dining room.

"Well?" I prodded him when we were on the street.

"Do you remember that I told you Hope's husband was a distinguished psychoanalyst who recorded his interviews on tape? Well, it's my hunch that sparked the whole thing."

"I don't understand what you are getting at."

"For a long time I've wondered, as everyone else does, how Lambert managed to get so many elusive celebrities on his program." When I stiffened, he said, "Wait! Give me a chance, Mattie. I'm not throwing any suspicion on Alan. I believe the guy was really in love with Kay and that he's shaken right down to his heels by her murder. No, the first time something really rung a bell was when you and I went to Hope's apartment."

"Hope!" I stood stock-still on the sidewalk until Hall's hand on my arm urged me on.

"Hold your horses, kid. Do you remember the first impression you get when you enter that apartment? The luxury. The unexpected luxury. The paintings. They were originals. Did you realize that? There's a small fortune in art on the walls of that living room. Now Hope makes a big salary, as I happen to know, but not that kind of money, not what might run into a quarter of a million dollars worth of paintings. And she's no art lover. I think they are an investment, one kind of stock that won't be at the mercy of the market. Hope's husband died broke, Mattie. He had nothing to leave her, which is why she took a job. Nothing except for those tapes."

"She destroyed them!"

"She told me she destroyed them."

"That is a perfectly filthy insinuation," I said, hotly. "Hope is the finest, the most loyal — why you've always said so yourself!"

"She's an astute business woman. And she's tough as a successful executive has to be. But really tough."

"I think she is the kindest person I have ever known, and the most understanding. You can ask anyone at the station."

"Cool it, Mattie. Just let me speak my piece. I never had a scrap of suspicion against Hope until I walked into that living room and saw the paintings."

"But a woman as clever and competent as Hope wouldn't need to do anything crooked, if that is what you are getting at."

"There are people who have a gambling instinct so strong that they'd rather take chances, hair-raising chances, than do the straightforward thing; driven by a gambler's blind faith in his luck and a kind of recklessness."

"She told me once that Scott Jameson is that kind of gambler."

"Did she? Well, this is the way I began to figure it out, Mattie. Hope was hard up when her husband died; he was much older than she, a whole generation older, and after his death she had no resources to fall back on. She got a minor job at the broadcasting station and pulled herself up by her own bootstraps to her present position. But way back there when her husband died I happened to meet one of his patients who told me about the experiment with tapes. That's when I tried to buy them, simply to use as a springboard for ideas for plays. But I told you about that. And that's when I think I planted the idea of their potential value with Hope."

"I don't believe you. It's not characteristic of her."

"You stay in there pitching, kid. Anyhow, I think she began to use them for blackmail and it was out of the proceeds that she bought that art collection, and she probably has plenty salted away, too. But she learned something more intoxicating than how to get money out of people. She learned how to create fear. She learned the meaning of power. It is my contention that she switched from forcing people to pay up or be exposed to forcing them to appear on Alan's program and dance to her tune, at the same time affording him immense prestige."

"If you can make yourself believe for one

minute that Alan would lend himself to such a scheme you're off your head."

"Actually, I doubt if he has an inkling of the whole thing. Face it, honey, he has a faculty for bowling women over, though what it is I don't know, but even if it's a surface charm, he has a genuine warmth and friendliness. I doubt if he could fake that. But remember, before Hope discovered him he had been contentedly playing the heavy in Grade B westerns for years. Pretty much the same part all the time and not much required of him but a few lines of dialogue, an ability to scowl in a menacing way, and to ride a horse."

"You make him sound like a fool."

"Well, he's no mental giant. That's for sure. That rugged appearance can be mighty misleading."

"And I suppose you know why Hope would go to such trouble to build Alan up."

"I leave that to you to figure out. He gets the women. Hope may have hooked him and then built him up. And all along the line there was excitement and risk."

"This sounds like one of your own plays — no, like one of those nightly thrillers you forget as soon as it's over," I said coldly.

"The most unkindest cut of all. So we drop theory and come to some proof. I'd been noticing for some time that Alan's big fish were not always happy on his program. That's when I thought of Clifton. You remember that broadcast? He acted like a trapped animal and Alan was taxed with all he could dredge up to keep the thing going for a full hour."

"I remember. Hope laughed and said it took some people that way."

"Yes, well, when I began to get this hunch of mine I thought of Clifton because I knew him. We had become close friends in college, one of those strange attractions of opposites, as I'm a confirmed introvert and he's the man of action. He was the one who had told me about being analyzed by Bancroft and the experiment with the tapes.

"So the other night, with suspicions getting stronger every day and nothing to back them up, I went to see him at that place of his on East End Avenue. We talked almost all night before I finally broke him down. He'd been blackmailed into appearing on the Lambert program. He didn't suspect Lambert himself but he knew someone at the studio must be rigging the thing. He was just about out of his mind with worry. It seems the poor devil had lost his nerve. He got to the place where he could hardly step off a curb without getting into a cold sweat, and here he was being built up everywhere as the man who feared nothing. Dr. Bancroft had straightened him out but someone got hold of those tapes and could have wrecked his reputation and made him look like God's most awful fake."

When I had nothing to say he went on, "So I began hunting around, checking back on the big names who appeared on the program. I met with a lot of rebuffs; some people wouldn't give me the time of day; some threatened me with the police, thinking I was in the game and attempting extortion; but I got to that big financier — remember? — and found out he made his start by stealing money from an old woman who had taken him out of an orphanage and brought him up. Afterwards he had repaid every cent with interest and looked after her until she died. Still — there it was.

"And the senator — that's not a pretty story. A queer kind of sexual deviation. He's got it all under control now, with Bancroft's help, but any rumor of it would ruin him and he's been a darned good public servant, whatever his private life is — or was. It all comes down to the tapes and only one person had access to them."

"Hope!" I said blankly. "Hope! But, Hall, she couldn't possibly — and Kay — she couldn't — and why would she?"

Hall shrugged. "I don't know. Did she want Alan for herself and wipe out the competition or did Kay find out what she was up to?" He checked his watch. "Better get back on the job. See you."

When I returned, the television screen continued to show the man who demonstrated cooking lessons, with the eternal breaks for advertising commercials — and before I die I hope I have a hand in exterminating the man who invented the singing commercial. And then Alan was on the air with a couple of schoolteachers who were debating the merits and demerits of teachers' strikes. They were so heated that Alan had little to do but put in a soothing word now and then to prevent a free-for-all. He looked awful. Even the make-up man had not been able to erase the ravages of sleeplessness and suffering. I could hardly bear to look at him. And when I thought of what would happen to him and his career if Hope's activities were ever exposed, it made me sick. He shouldn't be asked to take much more. He, like the rest of us, had trusted Hope blindly.

There was a break for a commercial and then the camera was back on the three people seated in front of the curtain with

Alan's name emblazoned on it. He leaned forward to speak to one of his panel, leaned farther and farther forward, and toppled at their feet.

Fourteen

Half an hour later Alan came out with Hope supporting him on one side and a cameraman on the other.

"I'm taking him to my doctor," Hope said as they went past. "I'll be back later; probably be at the station most of the night making arrangements."

Alan said nothing, shuffling between his two escorts.

For the rest of the afternoon I was frantically busy. It seemed that everyone in New York who had been watching the Alan Lambert show called to find out what had happened, to offer sympathy, to demand more information.

Phil Carmichael came in with as phony an air of sympathy as I've ever seen, but I couldn't blame him. After all, this was his big chance to prove himself.

I was just preparing to leave for the day, turning over the switchboard to my replacement, when Hope came back. "I took Alan to my own doctor who says he has to take a month off. He is at the breaking point and he can't stand the emotional tensions of doing five shows a week. I'll probably be here for the rest of the night, setting things up. God! Everything seems to come at once, doesn't it? Well, at least this will be Phil Carmichael's finest hour. He's waited for a break like this for more than a year."

"But, Hope, Alan will go out of his mind if he has to stay home, doing nothing, living alone in that house, without Kay."

"He won't be there. I've made up my mind to one thing. He's got to have a complete change. I'm arranging to send him out to Arizona to his friend Scott. Scott will know what to do."

As I was leaving, the other operator called me back. "Some man for you."

It was Lieutenant Saunders to say that the window had been repaired and bars put on and I could go back at any time. The place, he added, was a bit messed up, of course.

"I don't suppose you've remembered anything useful."

I told him then about Alan's collapse — "He's a sick man, Lieutenant; a very sick man" — and that he was going to take a month's leave of absence, on doctor's orders, and that he would probably go out to Phoenix.

I was so absorbed in my thoughts, the

shock of Alan's collapse and Hope's intention of sending him to Arizona, that when I left the station I automatically turned toward the apartment instead of Beekman Towers. It was odd that, in an emergency, I had forgotten all about Hall's accusations — or allegations — about Hope. She had been the one to come to Alan's aid, to get him to a doctor, to arrange for his leave of absence, to plunge into all the complex details of providing an adequate replacement during his absence while protecting his interests so there would be no difficulty about his returning.

Hall had been so convincing that he had — almost — made me believe him. Now I thought, with a lifting of the heart, that Hope was in the clear. She had always been in the clear. I remembered her ceaseless kindnesses not only to me but to anyone who needed her, like poor Angela, who had known that she could go to her for refuge in time of need. I thought of the way she had built her position at the station and the keen intelligence with which she tackled any job. Such a woman did not turn blackmailer. Such a woman did not condone or take part in murder. And never had I observed anything personal in her attitude toward Alan. He had referred to her as "the little mother of us all," which seemed to sum up adequately her position in his life as well as at the station.

And her art collection? Well, the fact that I had a certain facility at sketching, that I had a fairly good eye, did not indicate that I was an expert. The paintings might easily be copies. After all, recent and embarrassing discoveries had indicated that more than three hundred paintings acquired by the Metropolitan Museum with the approval of experts were not what they were purported to be. Hall could be mistaken.

I went down the basement stairs and fumbled in my handbag for the key, turning toward the light to see the contents, so my back was turned to the door that led into the main part of the basement.

The door to my apartment burst open and I was hurled aside like a cork shot out of a bottle and fell in a heap on the basement stairs. I tried to sit up, gasping for breath, and the gray-haired man leaped past me and up the stairs. And then Hall was bending over me. I don't know what made me close my eyes.

"Mattie! Mattie! Are you all right?"

I opened my eyes and saw him trying to lift me, saw the look of concern on his face. I struggled to get up.

226

"Where does it hurt?"

"I'm not hurt," I said crossly. "I wasn't exactly hit. Just pushed. Flung away from the door when that gray-haired man came barging out."

"I was here." Hall smiled at me. "No one else. Look here, honey, you're getting much too fanciful. That gray-haired man — you know the verse:

As I was going up the stair
I met a man who wasn't there.
He wasn't there again today.
I wish to God he'd go away!

Aren't you going to ask me to come in? Where are your manners, girl?"

"You saw that man and let him get away and now you are lying to me about him. Why?"

There was an odd expression on his face. "What do you think I'm trying to do? I'm looking after you the best I know how though I admit I'm not making a very good job of it."

"I don't believe you."

"But, Mattie —"

"I've had enough," I said fiercely. "I don't believe you. Please go away!"

After a little pause Hall did so, without

comment or protest.

I went into my apartment then and stood staring. "A little messed up," Lieutenant Saunders had said. The place was a shambles, like the rooms in Kay's house. Drawers had been overturned, kitchen stuff was spilled all over the place. My pretty rooms were a godawful mess. I took a long look at them and sat down and cried.

Then I dug out jeans and an old shirt and got to work. It didn't take so long, after all, to straighten up the living room or even the bedroom, though I didn't like the bars which made my gay little room look like a prison. But the kitchen was a sickening mess, with flour and sugar spilled over the counters and the floor and even on the walls, as though the canisters had just been dumped.

But had all this damage been done by the intruder of the other night or by the gray-haired man who had come bursting out of the apartment when I appeared? And what had Hall been doing there? I felt sick at heart and I worked as hard as I could, trying to drive out my tormenting thoughts and the questions to which I found no bearable answer.

There was only one thing I was sure about: for reasons best known to himself

Hall had lied to me. Lied and lied and lied. It was easy to see now that his apparently assiduous attentions had been a determined effort to check on me and my actions. Alan had been worried about Hall and had tried to warn me. Hope had tried her best to make me see the light. And she had been justified in pointing out my lack of sophistication. I had had so little masculine attention, except during that winter when I was alone in Boston, that I took it too seriously.

It was nearly half-past seven when I had the apartment in shape again, checked food supplies so that I could shop on my way home the next evening, showered and changed to the dress I had worn to work, and went out to get a hasty meal at a lunch counter and then back to Beekman Towers.

The desk clerk smiled at me. "Nice evening, Miss Pelham. Message for you."

It was a brief note from Mansfield saying he could not wait any longer as he had to pack for Mr. Lambert who was flying to Phoenix in the morning for a month.

Next morning it seemed odd to be going to work knowing that Alan would not make his customary spectacular appearance, followed by a horde of his fans. In fact, the whole tempo of the place seemed to be changed except for the feverish number of calls made by Hope, as she lined up guests for Phil Carmichael, briefed him on those already signed up, and carried on all her own routine multitudinous tasks.

Alan telephoned to say good-bye. He was feeling better, he said, but his voice sounded faint, without its usual confident ring.

"You'll rest, won't you?" I asked.

There was a thread of laughter. "God! I don't want rest. I'd like to spend eight hours a day riding on the desert. Say good-bye to Hope for me, won't you, Martha, and try to thank her adequately for all her kindness. I don't think I was up to it yesterday, and I know I'm causing her a hell of a lot of trouble by dropping out this way."

"Don't worry, Alan. Hope will manage."

And then he was gone and the day stretched emptily ahead.

As Hope was going out to lunch I stopped her to relay Alan's message. She nodded, frowning, and then smoothing out the wrinkles. "These big men who look so husky," she said, "and then break all of a sudden. But I honestly think he'll be all right, Martha. He's had a scare; probably thought he was indestructible. Well, we've got the situation under control here, at any rate."

"You have," I corrected her.

She smiled at me and then her eyes narrowed. "And what's wrong with you, Martha? Yesterday you were as bright and gay as a red tulip. Today you're all washed out. If it's Alan —"

I shook my head. "It's not Alan." When she waited, I told her about the gray-haired man who had been in my apartment and that Hall had lied to me, denying that he had been there.

Hope let out her breath in a sigh, squared her shoulders to meet this new burden, and said briskly, "That settles it. You are coming home with me. Oh, I can't make it for dinner. I've got a date with one of Alan's sponsors. I've got to reassure him that Alan is going to be all right and that Phil is perfectly competent to carry on. Matter of fact, if he is smart enough to be himself and make use of that boyish charm, instead of trying to imitate Alan, which he hasn't the personality or the maturity to do, he'll be fine. And after dinner I'll have to come back here to sign my mail." She dug into her handbag and pulled out a key.

"Let yourself in. The bed in the spare room is always made up for a guest. Make yourself at home, Martha. And don't worry about anything." She leaned forward to brush my cheek lightly with her lips, looked at the clock, and rushed out.

That afternoon I turned on the sound on the TV screen and watched how Phil Carmichael took over for Alan. Bitterly as I resented his having Alan's place I had to admit he did it well. He began with a brief but effective tribute to Alan, a man who had sustained a terrible tragedy in the brutal murder of his lovely wife, his bride of a few months. He had struggled valiantly to carry out his obligations until he had collapsed. His well-wishers, and they were many, looked forward to his recovery and return. Meanwhile, and Phil flashed his boyish smile, he would do the best he could.

When I was through for the day I went back to check out at the Beekman Towers and pack. I wondered whether Hall would try to get in touch with me, in spite of my rebuff, but at this point it did not seem to matter.

Because the rent for the hotel room had drawn heavily on the cash in hand I decided to walk to Hope's apartment. At first the suitcase wasn't heavy but before I got there I had to change hands frequently and stop to rest. It was when I bent to pick it up at a light that I thought I saw the gray-haired man again, but by the time I had crossed the street there was no sign of him. Anyhow, he couldn't get at me in Hope's apartment.

I let myself in, feeling like an intruder. The place was empty, of course. The woman who cleaned for her came in mornings. I found the guest bedroom, equipped with its own small bathroom and, with Hope's usual efficiency, thoroughly comfortable.

When I had unpacked I wandered back into the living room. The paintings were well lighted and I moved from one to another, studying them as closely as I could, but aware that I simply lacked the expert knowledge to estimate their authenticity. Certainly they looked all right. All right? They were magnificent and provided the thrill that comes with great art.

I wandered across the big room, skimmed the titles on bookshelves, picked up one of Jane Goodall's books, which I had missed, and tried to settle down in a deep, heavenly comfortable couch, to project myself into the life of that dedicated woman scientist in Africa. Heaven knows the material was fascinating enough but my attention kept straying.

By now Alan was in Phoenix. It would be warm there. The chances were that he would regain his shattered health if he really spent some time riding, as he planned.

All of a sudden I wanted to write to him,

to tell him how important it was for him to take good care of himself. On impulse I dialed Kay's house. When Mansfield answered I asked him for Alan's Arizona address.

"Mrs. Bancroft said he'd check in at the Desert Hills Motel until he got settled, Miss Pelham. Oh, and —"

"Sorry I forgot about you yesterday, Mansfield. I ran into a spot of trouble. Can you tell me now?"

"Not very well. You know where the phones are, miss. No privacy. But there's one thing. I took the liberty of calling the station to ask if you'd forgotten about me and got a lady who said she was your friend. And — she's the lady who called and said she was Mrs. Lambert. I'm absolutely sure. I knew as soon as she spoke."

"Well — uh, good night, Mansfield." I set down the telephone with nerveless fingers. Hope! It had to be Hope. But Hope could not have had a hand in Kay's death. Could not. But why would she have called the house, pretending to be Kay, leaving a garbled message to confuse Alan when he returned? But — if it had been Hope, then with whom had she been working?

I walked up and down the thick carpeting until, when I accidentally touched a silver cigarette lighter on the desk, it gave me an electric shock clear to my elbow and I dropped the lighter. It fell under the desk and I had to get down on hands and knees to retrieve it. That was when I saw the curious bulge under the edge of the desk and thought something had got stuck, caught in a drawer. It was one of those little hide-a-key boxes and the top slid open at my touch, so the key dropped on the floor. There was a tag attached to it, reading, "S.J." with a Jane Street address.

I don't know how long it took for the idea to register in my paralyzed mind. Hope and Scott. And Alan, at Hope's instigation, had gone out to Phoenix, walking into the waiting arms of Scott Jameson. Gone unarmed and unwarned, straight into a baited trap.

I stumbled to the telephone and, after the usual difficulties, got the telephone number of the Phoenix motel and then had to wait while they paged Alan. There was, I remembered a two-hour difference in time. At last the switchboard operator reported that Mr. Lambert did not answer the telephone in his room and he had been paged without result in the lobby, the restaurant, and the bar.

So he might already have got in touch with Scott! For a moment I thought of calling the Phoenix police and alerting them to his danger but there would be a terrific amount of publicity, given Alan's reputation and Kay's recent death, and anyhow I hadn't a scrap of proof to give them.

I felt in the hidden compartment in my wallet, probably known to every pickpocket in the business, and found two twenties and a ten-dollar bill. Not enough. Further search revealed the edge of a couple of fifty-dollar travelers' checks left over from my winter in Boston.

I walked to the corner before taking a cab as I didn't want the doorman at Hope's apartment to tell her where I had gone. Jane Street was in a part of New York I didn't know at all. The taxi driver found the number with some difficulty and then eyed me dubiously. "This where you want to go, miss?"

I nodded, paid him, and went up unswept steps to a door with dirty glass, which stood ajar. There were eight mailboxes in the little space between inner and outer doors and the name Scott Jameson hand-printed on a torn piece of cardboard. There was nothing in the mailbox. I tried the inner door but it was locked. After a moment's pause I rang three bells at random and the door clicked open.

Someone looked out from the back as I

went in. "Yeah? Looking for Helman?"

"Sorry," I mumbled, grateful for the low-watt bulb. "I forgot my key."

The woman grunted and slammed her door and I went up the stairs. Scott Jameson had the back apartment on the third floor. I knocked several times but there was no sound. And then, with my heart thudding, I slid the key in the lock and opened the door. Again I listened. Then I groped along the wall for the light switch.

It was a two-room and kitchenette apartment and I could see everything but the bathroom at a glance.

The furnishings were meager and shabby. In the kitchenette the shelves were empty except for a couple of bottles of Scotch and the refrigerator was humming but held nothing except ice cubes. This place was not lived in, as was confirmed by the bathroom where there were no toothbrushes, no toothpaste, no combs or brushes. Only a bar of expensive perfumed soap and a fine linen towel. The apartment had the air of being a poor man's love nest. There was a woman's dress and a man's suit in the bedroom but the dresser drawers were empty. I went back and looked in the bathroom hamper. Slowly, with the tips of my fingers, I lifted out an olive green wool jacket, which was drenched

237

and stiff with dried blood. It was a jacket I had seen Hope wear several times. Under it was a man's jacket with white marks along the sleeves and across the breast. Ammonia stains. And under that were two more towels, a rusty color, and encrusted with dried blood. Then I looked back at the washbowl. That at first had seemed to be streaks of rust must be blood washed off in haste.

Well, I had my proof at last! But why in heaven's name had Hope left this incriminating evidence? Then I realized that, believing her association with Scott to be unknown, she felt safer in leaving things as they were than attracting attention of the police by going there to retrieve the stained clothing. But the waiting must have been hell. No wonder she had aged.

I hunted through the apartment for a telephone but there was none. My first job must be to reach Lieutenant Saunders. Then I hesitated. If I called him, he would be bound to detain me until a search had been made of the apartment and I intended to be on the first flight for Phoenix.

I got out of the apartment as fast as I could. There was no cab in sight but I found myself running toward a corner drugstore where I bought a package of envelopes and some paper. Standing at a counter I wrote a note to Lieutenant Saunders, telling him what I had found in the apartment on Jane Street and enclosing the key. This, at last, was what Kay had known, what she had intended to tell Alan about his dear friend Scott, that he was secretly linked with Hope Bancroft.

I finished my note by saying, "Mr. Lambert has been lured into a trap. I can't reach him by phone. I'm taking the first plane."

I hailed a taxi and had the driver take me to the airport. By the time I reached Phoenix the New York police would have all the evidence they needed and perhaps they would even have Scott Jameson in custody. I sealed the envelope, and when I paid off the cabbie I handed him the envelope and a five-dollar bill.

"This must be delivered to the police station at once," I told him. "It's desperately important."

He looked rather blank but at least he could read and he seemed to be honest. "At once," I repeated.

Thirty minutes later I was airborne, headed west toward Arizona — and Alan.

Fifteen

It was late when I reached Phoenix and took a cab to the Desert Hills Motel. Only when I reached the desk did it occur to me that they might wonder at my having no luggage and then realized that they probably assumed I had driven.

When I had signed in I inquired, casually, about Mr. Alan Lambert. Not that I wanted to disturb him tonight, of course, but I'd like to leave a message for him. The clerk shook his head. Mr. Lambert had been there only a few hours while he got in touch with an old friend and then he had checked out.

"But I expected him to be here!" I exclaimed in distress. "He's my brother-in-law and I've been worried about him. He collapsed at the studio and —"

The clerk nodded. "We heard about Mr. Lambert's collapse. And, of course, we've been reading of his wife's terrible death. New York must be a pretty rough place to live in. All those muggings. I can't say I'd care for it myself And we have a special feeling for Mr. Lambert who is, as of course you know, an old Phoenician. He made a lot of movies out here not so long ago."

"Did he seem — is he all right?"

"I didn't see him myself," the clerk said regretfully.

"Do you know where he went?"

This took longer, but inquiries finally reached a young man who doubled as bus boy and driver of the airport bus. He'd seen a guy meet Mr. Lambert down in the lobby. Met like old friends. He'd driven Mr. Lambert off in a beatup pickup truck. He didn't know where.

"Can you describe Mr. Lambert's friend?"

The boy shrugged. There was nothing special. Dressed like half the guys out here: boots, jeans, red shirt, Stetson hat.

So, after all, Alan had fallen into Scott's hands as neatly as a piece of ripe fruit falling out of a tree, and I didn't know what to do next. My chief hope was that Lieutenant Saunders, having checked the apartment on Jane Street, had evidence now that Hope and Scott Jameson had been involved in Kay's murder. The next step was clearly up to him.

Having met Alan so publicly it was unlikely that Scott would do anything to him at once. There was nothing for me to do but go to bed.

241

In the morning I got my first impression of Phoenix when I walked through the pretty grounds, around a swimming pool, under rustling palms to the coffee shop in the motel. I had left my coat in my room but even so I was much too warm. The sky was a deeper blue than I was accustomed to, cloudless, and the sun blazed down on my head. The dress that had been right for early April in New York was much too warm here but I couldn't afford the proper clothes. In fact, I could not afford another night at the motel. If I could not find Alan in a hurry I'd be in real trouble.

After breakfast I went back to the big lobby where I found a clerk who was not busy and asked her about places where movies were made in Arizona. A lot of westerns were still being shot at Old Tucson, she told me, and now and then a director wanting a stunning background in color did a film at Oak Creek Canyon, and, of course, there were pictures shot out at Apacheland.

Her face brightened. "We had one of the actors who used to do westerns out there right in the motel yesterday. Alan Lambert. He's on TV now but it's a daytime show so I don't get to see him. I knew him the minute he walked into the lobby. Once out at Apacheland he gave me his autograph but, of course, he wouldn't remember that."

"Apacheland. Do they make movies there now?"

"Oh, sure."

"Would you know an actor named Scott Jameson?"

She shook her head, rather chagrined as she felt she had set herself up as something of an authority on the movies. "Sorry. That name just doesn't ring a bell."

"But Apacheland is where Mr. Lambert used to make his films?"

She nodded. I checked out of my room, fingered my remaining money, and then, though I lost prestige by doing it, I asked the Jack-of-all-trades who ran the bus from the motel to the airport for the name of a reliable pawnshop. It wasn't far and I was so interested in the streets of this southwestern city that I didn't mind the walk even in the unaccustomed heat. I pawned my mother's pearls for two hundred dollars though I knew they were worth a lot more than that, and then I rented a little drive-it-yourself car, got a map and directions and set out for Apacheland.

Most of the drive was unexpectedly dull, mile after mile of mobile home sales lots, seeking a market among the retired couples with their Social Security incomes. Mile after mile after mile. And all the time I was thinking desperately: You've got to be there, Alan. You've simply got to. And it wasn't altogether concern for his welfare, there was also considerable concern for my own. To find myself penniless and friendless in a strange town more than two thousand miles from home was no picnic.

And then the mobile homes were left behind and I was in the Mojave Desert, a rough, inhospitable land, which offered no welcome to man, no hope of comfort or food or shelter. There were monstrous cactuses, the saguaros, which stand like headless giants with outflung arms, looming forty feet into the sky.

And then there were the Superstition Mountains, jagged and rough and treeless, mountains in which wise men did not travel alone because too many had lost the way and died there. They weren't beautiful but they were exciting in a strange sort of way.

At last when I was sure that I had passed the sign I saw it: APACHELAND. An arrow pointed left to a narrower road, which eventually was a gravel road, then a deep ditch into which the little car lurched and valiantly clawed its way up, and finally a bleak looking building with a sign: STAGE ONE.

I parked in the sand where there were half

a dozen cars and a shabby pickup truck. Before I could open the door a man stopped me. "Sorry, lady. They're shooting. You can't go in now."

"How long?"

He shrugged. "No telling. Might break off any time. Anyhow, they'll be stopping for lunch about twelve."

"Twelve!" I said in dismay, looking at my watch.

"If you want to, you can go across the road. They put on a tourist show every coupla hours. Two bucks. Not much of a show but it will pass the time."

So I followed more arrows and drove over into another parking lot, found an empty space, and paid two dollars to a girl in a booth.

Beyond the narrow passageway I found myself on the street of a typical western town, western, that is, in the sense of a background for old western movies. There was the familiar hotel; the saloon with a wagon outside, a team of horses stamping restlessly; the general store with a pony tied at the hitching post; a church, and a row of houses. Only when I looked through an open door into the out of doors did I realize this was a two-dimensional world. This was the west of a hundred movies; it was real and it was all, like the door that opened on nothing, make-believe.

In a corral horses stood apathetically and a cowboy was swinging a saddle over the back of a pony. Half a dozen cowboys stood in a huddle in the middle of the street. I looked quickly at them but none of them could possibly have been Alan. They were all equally tall but they were leaner. Along one side, set back from the mock street, there were a few rows of benches and even at this early hour a group of tourists waited for the show to begin.

Apparently there was some hitch in the performance and the little crowd was getting restless. Tourists are always in a hurry, anxious to get to some place else. A spokesman for the cowboys cleared his throat and said, "Sorry, folks; there's a slight delay. We've run out of ammunition and had to send into town for it."

A couple of people grumbled and said, "Let's go. Just a tourist trap, if you ask me."

But I waited. I had to wait for Alan, if Alan was really there, watching his friend Scott acting on Stage One.

The cowboys were in a huddle again and there was obviously a difference of opinion. A skinny youth was arguing about something, his voice shrill above the deeper tones of the older men. A man with long white hair, a straggly beard, fireman-red suspenders holding up his blue jeans, came swaggering across the lot from the stage. He looked like all the old miners in past westerns.

"What's all the jawing about?" he demanded, in a voice that was much younger than his appearance.

"Gus wants to do the jump from the top of the saloon onto the wagon. He wants some feet of film to send across the road. You want to watch it, Scott. You've got a rival here."

Scott! I stared at the old man in disbelief.

"Trying to make like a stunt man?" Scott drawled.

The boy flushed under the ironical gaze of the men. "I know I could do it."

"Know how far it is? That's quite a drop, kid. And you don't land on your feet, you know. You're supposed to be dead."

"I've seen you do it often enough. Just give me a break; that's all I ask."

"It's not up to me. Go to the management." This was apparently a familiar joke because there was a good deal of laughter. "Only they've got insurance here and it don't apply to any green kid who wants to be a stunt man for thrills. No, don't yap at me. Save it for the management. And clear out now. We've got to get this show on the road."

A man came running with what appeared to be the missing blank cartridges and the men took their places, inside the saloon and the hotel and the general store. Swaggering down the street came the old miner stripped of beard and wig so that he looked thirty years younger. He pushed his way into the saloon with a bluster that indicated to the initiated that he was the villain of the piece, the western Bad Man.

And now down the street cantered a horse bearing a man with a six-shooter at his side, and a big sign reading SHERIFF. I didn't follow the action very closely. You've seen it a hundred times if you're an addict of western movies.

The Bad Man swaggered out of the saloon, argued with the sheriff, defied him, and then cowboys began swarming from all the buildings, aligning themselves on both sides. There was a wild and indiscriminate exchange of blank cartridges, no wonder they ran out of ammunition, and horses galloped onto the scene with a posse of armed men. The Bad Man, with a defiant gesture and after an exchange of shots, so many that it argued against anyone of them being able to hit a target at a foot's distance, rushed into the saloon and a few minutes later appeared on the roof.

The sheriff aimed at him, fired, and Scott, clutching his breast, staggered down the sloping side of the saloon, turned around a few times to give the tourists good value, and then half jumped, half fell into the wagon below.

Someone drove the wagon away. Then the sheriff, polishing his badge, raised his Stetson hat to the applause, so feeble as hardly to be heard, and rode manfully into the middle distance.

"That's all, folks. Next show in two hours," a voice boomed through a loudspeaker and Scott was back, carrying his wig and beard. "Anyone got a cold beer? I'm parched."

"Here you are, Scott," the kid said eagerly. "Just the same I could do it and then you wouldn't have to take a break every coupla hours to do this part."

"Ever try buying your own beer, Scott?" one of the cowboys suggested.

"He don't have to," another retorted. "His friend Lambert is here to pick up the tab. Some day he'll get wise to you for the deadbeat you are, Scott."

"Very funny," Scott commented. "Very funny."

There was a bustle and a little group, kicking up dust as they walked, came across the road from Stage One to a canteen that advertised hamburgers, hot dogs, pizzas, Coke, and cold beer. Now the tourists settled back with a little sigh of pleasure. For once they were getting more than they had paid for, a chance to see real live actors as they trooped over for lunch, most of the men in cowboy outfits, a man in a tail coat and silk hat, who played a gambler, a demure girl in a gingham dress and a sunbonnet, the local beauty, and one with a parasol, bustle and trailing skirt, so appropriate for the dust of the road, who was the eastern belle and rival to the simple maiden. There was a harassed-looking man in shirt sleeves, his hat pushed back on his forehead, talking earnestly to Alan, who looked a little larger than life size, even in these surroundings, his homely granite-like features providing more reality than all the rest.

And then I was running through the dust, calling, "Alan," and flung my arms around him.

For a moment he held me, an expression of sheer shock on his face. "Martha! What on earth —" Then he released me gently, tipping up my chin while he looked at me in concern. "You poor baby! What's gone

250

wrong? And why on earth did you come here? How did you find me?" He grinned. "I'm the most baffled man in Arizona at this point."

"Well, I had to talk to you and I didn't know just where to find you and there wasn't a minute to lose because you're in awful danger, Alan."

He stared at me. In this relentless sunshine I saw more clearly than before the ravages that Kay's death had caused him.

"And anyhow," I went on breathlessly, "I had to find you because I've simply got to have some money."

He looked at me as though I were a stranger. "Some money?" he said slowly.

"Well, at least enough for lunch and maybe if you could cash a check you'd lend me enough to get back to New York."

His face cleared then and he began to laugh. "Martha! You crazy child. Did you just come racing out here without a penny? Why on earth didn't you ask Hope? She could —"

"That's why I came." I clutched at his arm, aware now that we were the focus of attention. "Can't we get away from here? Away from all these people? It's terribly important, Alan."

He looked around rather helplessly and I

realized that it had always been Hope who arranged things for him. He caught the eye of the harassed-looking man. "Jake, this is my little sister-in-law, Martha Pelham; Jake Woods, the director of this horse opera."

"Take her over to my office, Alan," the director suggested. "No hurry. Kate caught the flounce of her skirt and has to mend it before she can go on anyhow."

Alan led me across the dusty lot and into the big bleak building with cameras and lights and a small space fixed up as a room in an old ranch house. I sat on a horsehair sofa, which took concentration to keep from sliding off, and Alan sat in an old-fashioned rocker with knobby arms.

"All right," he said, "let's have it."

So I started pretty much at the end, telling him about having discovered in Hope's apartment the key marked S.J. for an apartment on Jane Street. That was what Kay had found out, that Hope and Scott were shacked up there, and they were blackmailers. That was why they had had to kill her.

"For God's sake, Martha, you don't know what you are saying."

"And in a hamper in the bathroom I found a jacket of Hope's simply stiff with blood and a coat that must have belonged to

Scott and towels stained with blood.

"They killed her. They killed Kay. And then Hope was afraid you'd find out and she sent you out here to Scott. That's why I didn't dare wait. I just took the first plane out here to find you, to warn you."

"And you didn't speak of this to anyone?"

"There wasn't time. I wanted to telephone Lieutenant Saunders but I was afraid he'd make me wait while he searched the apartment for evidence."

"But why, Martha? You've let your imagination run hog-wild. Why? I know these people. They are incapable of the kind of thing you are suggesting."

So I told him about Dr. Bancroft's tapes and that Hope had used them first to get money, when she bought her paintings, and later for power when she had set up Alan's program.

All this time Alan had not moved, watching me, his eyes fixed, pushing up and down on his finger the green scarab ring which he always wore, as he said, for luck.

And I remembered Hope describing Scott when she had talked to him, the fixed eyes, the ring moving up and down on his finger. And I knew then. The picture had been so vivid, something she had really seen. But it had been Alan, not Scott. I closed my eyes, afraid he would read the knowledge in them.

And Alan said gently, "Poor kid! You poor kid! We'll work this thing out. I'll get you back to New York but there won't be a plane for hours. We'll take a look at the desert first. All right?"

Jake came in. "Alan, I hate to interrupt you but there are a couple of guys here from the morning paper in Phoenix. They want a story and some pictures of you. If you'd let them take some with the cast it would be mighty good publicity for me. It would only take a few minutes."

"Why, sure," Alan said with the warm smile that had made him so many friends. "Glad to. I'll be right back, Martha." He touched my cold cheek with his fingers, cold in spite of the heat of the day. "I'll bring you some lunch when I come."

As soon as the sound of voices had faded away I shot out of the place like juice from a squeezed lemon and headed straight for the mountains. There was simply no place else to go. I couldn't take the only road, where I'd be picked up in a couple of minutes. I was afraid of the desert with its snakes and poisonous lizards and all the horrors I had read about. And there was nothing left but the mountains.

I ran, crouching, until I was around a heavy boulder and then I began to scramble, moving from side to side, always trying to be concealed behind big rocks, feeling the stone under my feet blistering hot, feeling the crown of my head parboiled by the sun, the relentless sun.

I made a lot of noise scrambling over rocks, slipping, causing a downrush of pebbles and small rocks from time to time. I couldn't keep up that pace for long, of course, not going uphill, and I'd never tried to climb a mountain in my life.

Then I collapsed on a flat stone to catch my breath. I looked back but I could not see the movie lot, so it was a cinch no one could see me. But I heard the blare of a megaphone calling, "Martha! Martha! Where are you?"

The *you* went on echoing eerily for a long time.

All afternoon I climbed, walking, scrambling, slipping, pulling myself up, with no idea of the direction I was taking. Once in a while I heard voices on the mountains and then I hid, squatting down behind a boulder, afraid to stand up, though I am not very tall and the boulders were very big.

My stockings had ripped and the straps of my sandals had broken. My feet were bleeding and I felt that I could not move another step. Then the fear of what was behind me drove me on.

By the time the sun had set — so at last I knew which way was west — I was too tired to walk or crawl another foot. I was hungry and exhausted, my legs ached, my feet hurt unbearably, and I was thirsty, so thirsty it seemed to me I could not stand it another minute. And I was afraid. More than anything I was afraid.

I found as level a space as possible and curled up on a rock that was now cool, that grew colder as the night wore on. And the stars came out, thick and low, so low it seemed to me that I could reach them. And then I began to hear stirrings, rustlings.

So far as I knew, snakes do not come out at night, only when the sun is hot, but I wasn't prepared to accept this as fact. There were coyotes and mountain lions and other big cats in these mountains. God knew what else. There might be bears for all I knew.

And worst of all, there was Alan. Alan who had murdered Kay who adored him. Or had she known the truth about him at the end, known that he and Hope were lovers, partners in a particularly filthy blackmail game, with Alan hiding behind the name of his friend Scott Jameson? No, that couldn't be. Kay was laughing, Mansfield had said, that last morning. She could not have told Alan what she had learned. Or had she done so, challenged him? She was never afraid. She was always reckless. And at the end had she seen Alan's face when she had pulled that spray out of her pocket?

I would never know that. What I could not figure out was why Alan had been able to have an unbreakable alibi for the time of Kay's murder. He had been in sight of countless people from long before her death until long afterwards. Or had he? At the reception he must have moved around from person to person. It would have been easy for him to disappear for a while. And he could have changed his coat in the Jane Street apartment. No one would have noticed. He always wore a dark suit when he did his broadcast and one dark coat would look like another, unless a person had a special reason for noticing the change.

Why had Alan married Kay if he was so closely tied up with Hope? The Spaulding money, of course. An enormous coup if they could pull it off. A tremendous gamble but then Hope had been speaking of Alan when she described Scott's gambling instincts.

And all that meant that they had intended from the beginning that Kay was to die. I felt a fierce satisfaction that Kay, like her mother, had not intended to turn the bulk of her fortune over to Alan to enjoy with another woman. He must have suffered a devastating disappointment when he knew of that half-million dollar inheritance.

Queer how different everything looked in the light of my present knowledge. Alan's insistence on paying his own way, his refusal to be helped by Spaulding money, was clear now. No one was to be able to say that he used his wife's money. So everything fell into perspective. Hall had said he'd been looking at it upside down.

Hall! And I had run away, leaving no address. Even if he still wanted to help me he could not. But would he want to? He had lied about the gray-haired man. I knew now how Kay had felt. There was no one I could trust.

Now and then I slept in spite of the increasing cold and my burning feet and my hunger and thirst and unhappiness.

The last thing I thought was, So that is what Kay knew. She knew that Alan was Scott, or the other way round. She knew about his relationship with Hope. She must have got proof somewhere. That was her secret.

And the word secret was like the combination that opens the safe. I could hear her laughing as she said, "What a wonderful place to hide your secrets," and I knew where she had left the message for me, the message that Alan had tried so desperately to find, for which he had ransacked my apartment as well as Kay's rooms, for which he had tried to silence me forever with the poisoned chocolates.

Sixteen

I suppose most women share my irrational fear of darkness. All sounds become magnified. Danger lurks but you don't know where or what it may be. The lifting of the dark at dawn was a blessed relief.

The light came back swiftly and for a few minutes I lay where I was, curled up on a smooth stone with my cheek against another. I was cramped and cold and hungry and, above all, thirsty. My feet hurt so badly when I tried to stand on them that I cried out. All my muscles were sore from the unaccustomed strain of climbing the day before.

I collapsed on my stone again, looking around me. The Superstition Mountains are not high compared with others but the spectacle around me was completely baffling. I had no idea where I was or where to go, if I could manage to walk at all. I was surrounded by rugged peaks where no one could possibly find his way without landmarks of some kind. I remembered then the story of the Lost Dutchman mine, a fabulous lode of gold whose location was lost when the Dutchman died. Many men had disappeared while seeking the mine in these mountains. Even today people made up expeditions to hunt for the mine, but no longer did anyone attempt to go alone; they traveled in groups for safety.

One thing was clear. I was lost, utterly and completely lost. I had escaped from Alan but there was no escape from the ravages of thirst and hunger. I was going to die here and I hated it. I wanted desperately to live.

It seemed impossible that I could find my way back to Apacheland. My strength would run out long before I could reach there. Anyhow, Alan could not afford to let me reach there; somehow he would have to stop me. He had not let Kay live long after she discovered his secret.

Would it have saved me if I had told him of the letter I had written to Lieutenant Saunders? Once he knew the game was up would he throw in his hand? Probably not. He was a gambler and he believed in his luck.

I crouched on the stone, trying to weigh my chances. I remembered the reporters who had come to get a story and take Alan's picture. They would hear of the tempestuous arrival of Alan's sister-in-law and of her subsequent disappearance. They must have heard the megaphone calling me. How was Alan going to explain that? Would it work for me or against me?

By this time Lieutenant Saunders must have discovered the evidence in the Jane Street apartment and he would probably get in touch with the Phoenix police. Why hadn't I had sense enough to leave word at the motel about where I was going? Whatever happened to me was my own stupid fault, which was small consolation. Or perhaps the taxi driver had never delivered my letter to the police. But I could not bear to think of that possibility.

I couldn't remain where I was. Anything was better than inaction. I'd just get hungrier and thirstier and stiffer. At length I started down the side of the mountain, heading east in the direction of the rising sun. It wasn't all downhill, of course; it meant going up and down, climbing over and around rugged slopes, forcing my way through rough bushes that fought back every inch of the way. This time I wasn't doing any running; I could barely put one torn, bleeding foot in front of the other. At least I made myself keep walking, no matter how much it hurt.

At last I took off my dress and removed

my slip, which I tore into strips with the help of a tiny pair of scissors I found in a small manicure purse kit. This was an unbelievably slow and difficult job but at last I had thick folds of nylon in which to wrap my feet and cushion them a little from the rough ground. After that, walking was a trifle easier.

As the sun rose higher I began to feel the heat. At first it was a grateful warmth that took the chill out of my body and made my muscles feel a bit more limber. Then there was the relentless sun beating on my uncovered head, brilliant light that dazzled me, and thirst that made it difficult to swallow and impossible to moisten parched and swollen lips. And the combination of heat, lack of sleep and hunger made me dizzy.

I kept an uneasy eye out for snakes, not really knowing what to expect, but at least I didn't worry about the big cats. Mountain lions do most of their prowling by night and anyhow they aren't apt to attack a human being without provocation, and heaven knows my last desire was to provoke them.

When I first heard the sound I didn't recognize it. Then I knew it for what it was, a helicopter, which seemed to be moving back and forth, very slowly, very low. Looking for something. Looking for me! I was sure of it;

from almost complete despair and defeat I was suddenly buoyant with hope.

Now I could see it, my eyes half closed against the blinding brilliance of the light, and I waved my arms frantically. It went past, leaving me behind, and I never knew a worse moment in my life.

If only I had had some way of attracting its attention. There weren't many possibilities so I stripped off my dress again, thanking heaven that it was a light color, leaving only panties and bra. When I heard the 'copter coming back, I climbed on the highest point I could reach, and waved my dress like a flag. Then, once more, the 'copter was out of sight. No, it was turning. I waved again, screaming, though I knew no one could hear me above the noise of the motor. The 'copter passed, turned, came back, moved on, but this time I knew it was not leaving me; it was seeking a place to land. And then it settled some distance beyond me and a man was running, shouting, "Miss Pelham!"

It was the man with the gray hair. As I turned to make my escape I stumbled and fell over a bush and went sprawling, but this time I just lay there. I was licked. I tried to press myself further into the ground, a pointless business, but I had no place else to go.

"It's all right, Miss Pelham. You're safe now. You're with friends." He bent over me but he did not try to touch me. He raised his voice. "This way, Canfield. She's in pretty bad shape and I think she's afraid of me."

And then Hall was scrambling up the side of the mountain and scowling at me. "You could have got yourself killed, girl!" he stormed. "You know how many people get lost on these mountains? Sheer luck that we managed to find you."

"I resent that," the young pilot said, grinning. Then he got a good look at me and his grin faded. "My God! Oh, my God! What happened to her?"

"You can see what happened to her. She's half dead with exhaustion, her feet are torn to ribbons and she's marked all over from scratches and bruises and bleeding and —"

"First of all, she needs water," the pilot said, and I could hear his feet thudding as he ran back to get a thermos of ice-cold water. Nothing ever tasted as delicious as that did when he held it to my lips and Hall lifted me so I could drink.

"That's enough," the pilot said, in spite of my protests. "More later. Don't want to make you sick," and he pulled the thermos away from my clutching hand.

Hall and the gray-haired man carried me

down to the 'copter. "What we need," Hall said, "is a doctor." He sat with his arm around me, my head on his shoulder. He indicated the gray-haired man. "This is Burt Johansen, an ex-cop recommended by Lieutenant Saunders, who has been keeping an eye on you for me."

Burt shook his head. "I'm afraid I'm not so hot as a detective. You've spotted me almost every time."

"But why?" I asked Hall.

"After what happened to Kay and then that box of chocolates so nicely decorated with strychnine," as I shrank against him his arm tightened reassuringly, "I figured you needed more protection than I could give. So I asked Saunders about it and he recommended Burt, who left the force because of ill health and now enjoys an easy life."

Burt was amused. "Well, that's one name for it. Fortunately, I was following you when you went to Mrs. Bancroft's. I nearly spoke to you when I saw the struggle you were having with that suitcase. I figured you were all set for the night. And I was just about to make my report to Canfield and call it a day when you went down to Jane Street. When you came streaking out of there to get a plane for Phoenix, I just had time to call Canfield and I got a seat on the same plane.

That time you were too worked up to notice me."

"If you'd seen what I saw there —" and I told them. I've never had a better audience than when I described the evidence I had found: the blood-soaked clothing and the towels with which a hasty attempt had been made to get rid of what Lady Macbeth had called "the filthy witness."

The pilot commented, "I can't figure why they would leave such incriminating evidence behind?"

"Time," Burt said. "After the murder Lambert had to get back to that reception and circulate to show he'd never been away, talking to as many people as possible, and hoping to God he hadn't been missed. Mrs. Bancroft had to drive the body to the parking lot, which must have been a nightmare for the woman, no matter how hardboiled she may be. Broad daylight! The chances the two of them took! And after the murder neither of them dared make a single move, in case they were under observation."

"And may I ask what brought you out here like a bat out of hell, instead of going to the police like a sensible girl?" Hall demanded. He sounded so cross that I would have thought he disliked me if it hadn't been for that comforting arm around me.

"Alan," I admitted. "I didn't know then. I thought all the time it was Scott Jameson. I assumed Alan was in danger and Hope had shipped him off to Scott to dispose of."

"He's in danger, all right," Hall said, his voice ugly.

"You were right about Hope," I said magnanimously. "Did you know about Alan, too?"

"I guessed."

"Why didn't you tell me?"

"Would you have believed me? You were besotted with the guy. But, my God, after this I hope he burns. I'd hate to bet on it, though. He's popular and plausible and people believe in him."

"Don't worry," Burt said. "We've got plenty on him. If Lambert and the Bancroft woman were shacked up on Jane Street the chances are they left hundreds of fingerprints. Bound to. And Lambert's got a lot of explaining to do about breaking into Miss Pelham's apartment."

"Alan!" I exclaimed.

"The night I got you safely into the Beekman Towers," Hall said, "Burt was free to take a look at Lambert's activities and he saw the whole thing, jimmying the window, the works."

"And what were you trying to do yesterday afternoon when you nearly knocked me over?" I asked indignantly.

Burt grinned. "Sorry if I hurt you; I was in a hurry. Canfield and I hadn't expected you to go there and I was looking for the thing Lambert had failed to find."

"What would have happened," I asked in a small voice, "if I had been in the apartment when Alan came?"

"Well, you weren't. Don't think about it. He wouldn't have hurt you, Mattie. Look how hard he tried to get you to stay away from the place."

"Is he the one who tried to get in the night you were there?"

"I think so but I can't prove it."

"Why did you lie to me about Burt?"

"I thought it might make you nervous thinking you had a bodyguard."

"Nervous! Between the two of you, you scared me half to death. I didn't know whom to trust."

"Do you now?"

I nodded, afraid to speak, afraid to say how glad I was that Hall was there, to betray my feelings when I didn't know his feelings for me. At least not for sure.

"How did you find me?"

"Burt kept me informed. He was right on your tail all the time until you did your vanishing act into the mountains. As soon as I got to Phoenix I found his messages and hired the helicopter." Hall's arm tightened so hard it hurt my already bruised body. "That was the longest night of my whole life. I guess I'm going to have to put you on a leash to keep you from pulling any more tricks. The old man's getting to an age when he needs his sleep." His voice was light but his face was grim. "What made you run like that?"

"Realizing that it was Alan who had killed Kay. It hit me like lightning. And he said he was going to take me for a look at the desert before he sent me home and then some reporters came to see him and I started running."

"But why the mountains, for God's sake. The pilot tells me people get lost there all the time."

"Where else?" I demanded.

The 'copter settled gently on the ground and Hall lifted me out and carried me to Stage One. No one ever had a more colorful reception committee: the cast of the western movie in costume, reporters and cameramen from Phoenix, a group of tourists who had edged their way in to get a thrill for their money, several uniformed policemen and a tall man who looked like an army officer out of uniform.

There was a murmur of horror when we appeared and I heard one of the cowboys curse softly to himself. Later I saw some of the pictures taken before a nurse in the emergency ward of a hospital had cleaned and patched me up and made me look more human. I was in bra and panties and barefooted. My feet, from which the bandages had fallen, were torn and bleeding. My arms and legs were scratched and bruised, and my knees were scraped. My face, particularly my mouth, was swollen. My hair was a tangled mess.

When I observed the direction of the men's eyes I remembered that I was practically naked, and one of the actresses ran to get me a dressing gown, which I slipped on gratefully, tying it close around my waist.

The pilot of the 'copter again let me drink some of the precious water, this time almost enough, but again he took away the tempting flask before I could drink all I wanted, all my dehydrated body required.

And then Alan was there, his face alight with relief, coming with open arms. "Martha! Thank God! You've had us all in a dither and raised a lot of hell for one small girl."

Before he could touch me Hall and Burt were between us. Alan looked from me to

Hall. "What are you trying to do, Canfield?" He turned again to me, his one sure card, the besotted girl who had been infatuated with him from the first time she met him. "Martha! What happened to you, dear? What made you run like that?"

Then the tenderness was gone. "Surely," he exclaimed, more hurt than angry, "you didn't mean it when you demanded money of me? I thought you were joking. I thought — it's not like you, Martha. And when I refused to pay — what kind of game is this? It can't be because I wasn't in love with you, Martha. That can't be it."

I could feel color rushing into my face. I knew then just how much effect Alan would have on the witness stand. I had never before realized how good an actor he was. Every single person in that room was on his side. Every single one. If this had been the old west I'd probably have been lynched then and there.

Scott Jameson elbowed his way into the room and through the crowd, as typically a western figure as you could imagine, from the boots and tight jeans and loud shirt to the Stetson hat firmly riveted on his head, as though he never removed it.

"What's going on here? Why you trying to pick on Alan? He's a prince, that guy. A prince. The best friend a man ever had."

"Who are you?" This was the first time the tall man who looked like an army officer had spoken.

"Scott Jameson, if it's any business of yours."

"So you're Jameson. How long have you known that Lambert was renting an apartment in New York under your name?"

Alan was jolted by the unexpected question, shaken by the realization of what it meant. His eyes had a curiously fixed look and he pushed the green ring up and down on his finger. His color was ebbing away and his breath came quicker, more shallow. For the first time he was aware of the net closing around him; he felt the breath of danger on his cheek. Something had gone horribly wrong.

"There's nothing in that," Scott scoffed. "Just an old joke, kind of. Using my name, I mean. Used to be like an alibi. Whenever Alan wanted an excuse to go somewheres he said he was going to be with me because I needed him for something. We always got a laugh out of that." He went on, warming to his task. In his eagerness to protect Alan he failed to see the look Alan was giving him, trying to will him to be silent.

"Why it's been going on since we were

kids. I've covered for him over and over, especially when he wanted to get into a poker game or shoot a little dice and his folks thought he was too young, getting into bad company, bad influence, all that. And Alan was always mighty nice about giving me a share of his winnings. I got so I put it all into travelers' checks. Easy to carry around and I wasn't as apt to spend it as I would cash." He laughed heartily. "My old age security, huh?" He looked around, expecting them to share his amusement.

The big man asked, "Did Lambert tell you why he was hiding out under your name?"

"Hell, he wasn't hiding out. He's a big shot in New York now and people recognize him when he goes around so when he wants a little fun and games, know what I mean — and who don't, now and then? Tell me that." Scott looked around him triumphantly as though he had made a telling point.

"Mr. Lambert kept you informed about the use he was making of your name, then." This was the army type again.

"I don't know what business this is of yours," Alan said.

The tall man pulled out his credentials. "Lieutenant Campbell, New York Police Force." He added, "Homicide. I've been sent out here to take you back to New York."

Alan's hand groped for the back of a chair for support but he held himself upright. "What for?"

"The murder of your wife, Mrs. Alan Lambert, formerly Kay Spaulding, and I must warn you —"

"Kay! My beautiful Kay! You must be crazy, man. I was mad about her. What conceivable reason would I have had?"

It was Hall who intervened. "I'll tell you why. Kay hired a detective to find out about this Scott Jameson who claimed so much of your time, and he discovered the Jane Street place where Jameson was supposed to live and discovered that it was a hideout for you and Hope Bancroft."

Lieutenant Campbell, to my surprise, did not attempt to stop Hall. He simply stood at ease, looking from face to face, waiting, but prepared, I thought, for any sudden move.

"This is criminal nonsense, Canfield. I could sue you for slander and, by God, I'm going to do it. You've been out to get me ever since I married Kay when you wanted her and she wanted no part in you. A guy with a grudge. Because Kay and I had a marriage that was — so damned wonderful!" His voice shook with feeling and I was aware of the audience reaction. It was with him every step of the way.

"A wonderful marriage. And particularly all that wonderful Spaulding money. It was a hell of a gamble, Lambert, but it didn't pay off, did it? Having to wait until you are sixty to collect. That must have hurt bad."

Angry color flashed across Alan's face and ebbed again. He was still in full control. He looked from Hall to me, the jealous discarded suitor and the woman scorned, more with pity and bewilderment than with anger. Every moment he was gaining more support from his audience and he knew it. Every moment their opinion of Hall and me went down. He knew that too. But still inside of him something must have been screaming, wondering what had been found in the Jane Street apartment, whether Hope had been able to get there before the police.

"I have a fairly good job," he said quietly, knowing the value of understatement. "I'm making seventy-five thousand a year right now and I expect to be making four times that much by fall on a prime-time show. In another two years I should be right at the top, the over-a-million class. I didn't need Kay's money and as for Hope — why, man, she's one of the most brilliant women executives in Manhattan. She didn't have to do anything criminal in order to succeed."

"You are gamblers, Lambert, both of you; it's in your blood. But you had sense enough to know you can't always win and you wanted to make one big coup and get out. Marry the Spaulding money and then eliminate Kay."

"That's not true! There's nothing I like better than my job and if there's any honesty in you, Martha," and he turned to me abruptly, "you'll admit I never took a penny from Kay. Why I'm worse off than before I married her because I carried my full share of our expenses."

"Why not?" Hall said. "You were working for the jackpot. But now I can see you wanted to go on into the big time, but Hope was the one who wanted you to quit, she wanted you to quit while you had a whole skin. She has always been the one with the brains. She knew how easily you could crack under strain, as you cracked after Kay's murder. It wasn't as easy as it seemed, was it, Lambert? Stabbing in the back a woman you had made love to so often, stabbing deep down, feeling her blood warm on your hands, spurting out on Hope's jacket. Did she cry out? And getting her out to that car. Now that must have been quite a moment. Did you carry her or did you pretend to be supporting a drunk?"

No one in the room seemed to move, nothing but the green ring sliding up and down, faster and faster.

"And yet in a way it was Kay's victory. I'll bet when she confronted you and Hope and told you what she knew about you she laughed."

"No!" Alan needed someone like Hope to write the script for him.

"What were you looking for, Lambert, the night you jimmied the window in Mattie's apartment and ransacked the place?"

"I didn't."

Hall indicated Burt. "He is a private detective I hired to protect Mattie after you sent her those poisoned chocolates. He was following you the night you did your breaking and entering act. What were you looking for?"

I broke in. "I don't know what it is but I know where it is." I described the storage space behind the kitchen pipes and explained that no one could find it except as Kay and I had, by losing balance and grabbing at the wall. "Kay told me it was a good place to hide secrets. Whatever she left I can find."

"Oh — God!" Alan hardly breathed the words but in them was the despair of the gambler who has lost the last throw of the dice.

Seventeen

The next few hours were a blur. Alan went away with Lieutenant Campbell to New York. Hall drove me to a hospital where I was patched up and put back together again, while he went out to buy me a dress to replace the ragged one, a gorgeous thing I could never have afforded, and a pair of men's felt slippers at least three sizes too large, because I could not get my lacerated feet into shoes.

Then he and Burt and I made statements to the police and were given the pleasing information that we'd have to give much more detailed statements to the New York police. Alan, they told me, had been extradited to New York to face a murder charge. He had not put up a fight. He had gone along quietly enough.

"Just the same," Hall remarked, when the three of us were flying back to New York, "I'll bet my last dollar that Lambert still thinks he has an ace in the hole."

"If you can figure out what it is you're way ahead of me," Burt admitted.

"Hope Bancroft. From the beginning she's been the brains behind this operation. Lambert has absolute faith in her. He probably still expects that she'll pull a rabbit out of her sleeve."

"But how, married to Kay, so beautiful, could he look at another woman? Hope is pretty enough but, compared with Kay —"

"Kay was beautiful," Hall admitted, "the most beautiful woman I've ever seen. But Hope is all woman. Any man would notice that. There wasn't a lot behind Kay's beauty; that is, she could attract love but I doubt if she could return it. What she loved was the attraction she had for other people."

"But she was mad about Alan."

"She liked getting a man whom other women wanted. But Kay could never replace Hope, not in a million years. Hope and Lambert had too much in common; not just sex, though that was probably a powerful bond, but they are two of a kind, gamblers living recklessly for the sheer excitement of it. And then Hope developed a lust for power. There's no intoxication like it. No dope addict is ever hooked so completely. Look at the men of great fortune who go on accumulating. They can't spend it. They simply love the power to manipulate men or even governments. And the very danger involved in using those tapes Hope got from her husband added to the excitement and the challenge. Reckless? Kay had that reputation but, in comparison with Hope, she was Rebecca of Sunnybrook Farm."

It was late when we flew over New York, which had never looked so beautiful to me, that great glittering mass of lighted towers between two dark rivers, a proud and triumphant city. Hall carried me down the ramp from the plane and we were met by Lieutenant Wilkins and the big detective who accompanied him like a bulky shadow.

"What's wrong with the lady?" Wilkins asked.

Hall indicated the felt slippers and explained that my feet were still too painful to walk on. And why, he wanted to know, the reception committee.

"Lieutenant Saunders wants us to go to this young lady's apartment and see whether she can find a message of some sort from Mrs. Lambert. Then we'd appreciate it if she will go with us to the Jane Street apartment. Of course, the lieutenant and the crew have gone over it pretty thoroughly but there are a few questions, and it would be more practical on the spot."

"Not tonight," Hall said firmly. "Do you

281

know what time it is? After one o'clock? And Miss Pelham has had a rough time of it the past few days. She spent last night lost on a mountain."

"Certainly tonight," I said with equal firmness. Hall had no right to order me around. Not yet, at any rate. As for the future, it might all depend on how he felt about a girl who up to a few hours ago had thought she was in love with another man? And how did you go about telling a man that this time it was for real?

A police car, unmarked for a change, took us to my apartment where, at my direction, Lieutenant Wilkins climbed on the ladder, groped for the storage space, pulled out the plastic raincoat I thought I had lost and a thick envelope on which Kay had scrawled in her large writing: "Keep this for me, Martha, until I can explain. Until then *do not open*. I'm still not sure just how I intend to handle this."

"I want to read it first," I told Lieutenant Wilkins. "It was meant for me. If it has anything to do with all this I'll give it to you."

Reluctantly he surrendered the envelope and I ripped it open. There were half a dozen typewritten pages and a few snapshots. I skimmed the report hastily. Artur Antonelli had discovered the apartment of

Scott Jameson on Jane Street. The superintendent knew nothing about his tenant or how he earned his living but the rent was paid promptly each month in cash with an extra month in advance as security.

The superintendent had an idea that the couple was not married, as they occupied the place very rarely but as they were always quiet, no loud voices or parties or television, there was nothing to complain about. The Jamesons had occupied the apartment about four months. Usually they came together but occasionally the lady was alone. The superintendent, who seemed to take a serious view of his responsibilities, refused to admit the detective so that he could search the apartment.

Getting pictures had been difficult because there was no telling when the Jamesons would come so Antonelli had been staked out on Jane Street for some time. However he managed to get several shots of Hope and one of Alan, taken from behind so his face was not visible, but his carriage and the way he held his head were unmistakable.

Antonelli said that he had followed "Mrs. Jameson" to the broadcasting station where he learned her identity, an executive named Mrs. Hope Bancroft. The man he had been able to follow only once and he had admitted himself with his own key to Mrs. Alan Lambert's house. Did she want him to continue his surveillance?

"I'll bet Kay told Lambert she had a full report from Antonelli which she'd left with Martha," Hall said.

"But," I pointed out, "if she did that Alan wouldn't have dared to kill her. He'd realize that Kay's report from her detective would give him away. And the detective would speak up as soon as he heard of her death."

Wilkins gave a startled exclamation, said "May I use your telephone?" and without waiting for a reply he dialed headquarters. "What's the name of that private eye who fell or jumped in front of a subway a few days ago?" He waited. "Who? Sure of that? Yeah, I remember the tie-up of traffic. Commuting time. Yeah."

When he turned around his voice was hard. "These people work fast. Antonelli was a good guy, a good record, no trouble with the police, never held out on us. He got shoved in front of a subway train the afternoon Mrs. Lambert was killed."

"But it couldn't have been them. Alan must have had to go straight back to that reception."

"So it leaves the lady."

"I hope to God," Hall said, "that Lambert was allowed to call a lawyer. I don't want any hitch in this business because he failed to get his legal rights."

"There won't be any hitch," Wilkins assured him. "Mr. Lambert was allowed to make a call. He called Mrs. Bancroft."

"When was this?"

"Oh, at once, as soon as he was brought into the precinct." There was the suspicion of a wink. "Unfortunately Mrs. Bancroft's telephone was temporarily out of order. So then he called a lawyer." Wilkins turned to me. "Miss Pelham, will you go down to Jane Street with us? We'd like you to indicate just how you found things."

I agreed over Hall's brusque refusal— "It's two o'clock, man, and this girl has had it" — so of course he came along, carrying me out to the police car. On the way to Jane Street Wilkins told me that Mansfield had got hold of the police. He couldn't reach me, he said, and he felt he should tell someone. On the morning of the day she died Mrs. Lambert had spoken over the telephone to someone, saying, 'And be sure to bring your husband, Scott Jameson. Alan says I'll like him.' He thought it might be important."

"Then why didn't he tell Alan?"

"Mansfield," Hall told me, "knew Kay all her life and through all three marriages. If things were going wrong he'd know the symptoms."

When we got to the Jane Street apartment, Wilkins unlocked the door and made sure the blinds were closed before he turned on the lights.

"This the way you found it?"

I looked around. "There wasn't anything — wrong except in the washbowl and the clothes hamper in the bathroom. Only — I sort of remember another chair like this one."

Wilkins gestured for me to be silent and went to switch off the lights. There were feet on the uncarpeted stairs and I heard a man say, "It's okay for once, Mrs. Jameson, so long as it doesn't happen again. These things happen. I tell my wife she ought to wear her key around her neck. Half the time the neighbors have to take her in. Some time she's going to come home and no one will be there and then what will happen to her? But she never got anyone up at this time of night and I need sleep like anyone else."

"But I told you it wasn't necessary to come up with me."

"I'm paid to look after this place. I'll have a duplicate key made for you in the morning. Doesn't Mr. Jameson have one?"

"That's just it. He's had to go out of town on a new job and we're letting the apartment go, so I wanted to pick up our things tonight because I'm taking an early plane in the morning. I'll make sure the door is locked when I leave and I'll drop the key in your mailbox."

"Well, all right. Sorry we're losing you and the rent still has a coupla weeks to run. Good night." The superintendent yawned and stumped down the stairs.

And then the key clicked in the lock, the door opened and closed, the lights went on. Hope stood there, a suitcase in her hand, looking from me to Hall to the two policemen. The shock seemed to stun her.

Then she came forward and sat down, pulling off her gloves. You could almost see her thinking, gathering her wits. "Well, Martha. How did you get in here and where have you been?"

"I got in with a key I found in your apartment, marked S.J. and with this address."

"So?" She seemed to be making and discarding various approaches. At last she looked at the two big men with Hall. "I can't imagine what you are doing here unless you represent the Vice Squad. If you want evidence that Alan and I are lovers and that he

287

took this apartment in the name of Scott Jameson, it's all right with me. I'm not an untutored girl; I've been a widow for four years. Kay threw herself at Alan's head. It was a mistake for him to marry her, of course, but he's so darned soft-hearted. And now the poor devil is shattered by her death. He feels guilty because he wasn't faithful to her, though in the long run it would have made no difference, as she was mugged. I hope you won't bother him until he is able to come back to New York."

"Mr. Lambert is in New York," Wilkins said. He showed her his credentials. "He was brought back here to face a charge of first-degree murder of his wife."

Hope caught her breath in a sharp gasp. "No! That's impossible. Alan was in full sight of hundreds of people all day when Kay was killed."

"Let's not waste time, Mrs. Bancroft. You might as well know how things stand. Miss Pelham found incriminating evidence in this apartment, evidence which is now in the hands of the police laboratory. We have found a number of your fingerprints, and Mr. Lambert's — and Mrs. Lambert's on the arms of a chair which is now at the lab. From its condition we assume she was sitting there when she was stabbed."

These disclosures came like a series of blows. The hour was late and Hope had been under increasing strain and enormous emotional pressure. She sat dazed, trying to pull herself together, to turn defeat into a winning hand. She did not move except to clasp her hands so tightly that her fingertips were bloodless.

"We have also found Mrs. Lambert's missing jewelry, tying you in with the so-called mugging. And we have your husband's tapes. I suppose you had to keep them handy for constant reference in selecting new victims. We also have the report of Artur Antonelli which you tried so desperately to find, and which led to the poisoned chocolates, which were to eliminate Miss Pelham before she could find the report for herself. It's been a busy week, hasn't it?"

Hope made no reply.

"We've got you and Lambert sewed up as tight as a drum. You might as well make it easier for yourself and all concerned by cooperating."

Wilkins turned to his companion. "Go down and telephone for a police matron, will you?" He turned to Hope. "Hope Bancroft, I arrest you for complicity in the murder of Mrs. Alan Lambert and I must warn you that anything you say may be held against you. I regret that I cannot charge you with the murder of Artur Antonelli, though there's no question in my mind of your guilt. He was a good guy and he deserved better than that. As soon as the matron arrives we'll be going to the precinct."

Hope stirred at last. "What are they doing to Alan?" That was all that mattered to her. She was an unscrupulous woman, an evil woman, but she loved Alan exclusively, more than herself. While Alan was safe she would fight; if he was lost she had nothing left to fight for.

"They are asking questions. Showing him the strength of our case against him. Making him understand that nothing in God's heaven can get him out of this, not the smartest lawyer in Manhattan. He'll break, Mrs. Bancroft. He'll break."

"Yes, I know." She seemed almost indifferent. Gradually the tightly clasped hands relaxed, lay open loosely on her lap. "I don't know whether we held the wrong cards or we played them wrong. It was such fun in the beginning. Some of the stuff on those tapes my husband left was dynamite. Really dynamite. And I made money out of them. How I made money! I put it into those paintings because the market was jumpy."

Wilkins's companion had returned as soon as he had made his call, and he was taking down Hope's statement.

"It was you, Hall, such a monster of rectitude, who gave me the idea of using the tapes. It never occurred to me until then that they would have any value. So I began listening to them." She laughed. "You think Alan and I should be punished. You ought to get a load of some of the things America's big celebrities have been up to.

"And then I met Alan and that was the best thing that ever happened to me. I took a winter vacation and went to Las Vegas like a homing pigeon and Alan was there, also on vacation. I knew from the beginning what possibilities he had. A guy like that was wasted in westerns. So I began to think of how he could be built and then it occurred to me that there was another way of using those tapes. Instead of just getting money, why not force some of these big hard-to-get boys to appear on a program, which would send its rating sky-high, and they've been jumping through hoops because I liked it that way.

"It might have gone on until Alan had his prime-time show but now and then I could see that Alan was getting worried. He was afraid that some day we'd be exposed. So I figured we'd make one big coup, get out, and retire to some place like Switzerland. Well, Kay Spaulding met Alan and went overboard so that was the chance. The Spaulding money.

"I didn't think the marriage would last so long. But Alan kept putting off — anything final. She was beautiful and then she lived in a way he had never known before. Oddly enough she was responsible for it when it happened. She called me at the station to say she'd had a detective look up Mr. Scott Jameson. She suggested I meet her at the Jane Street apartment, and bring along my husband. Alan had always said she would like him. And she laughed!" Hope's small hands curled into claws.

"Well, the biggest break was that, though we had had no chance to plan, Alan had a wonderful cover. He would do his regular broadcast and then he was attending that big reception for Cosgrave. I didn't see how he could possibly be suspected, even for a moment.

"Well, I came down to Jane Street and admitted Kay. God, how arrogant she was! How amused. Like a cat at a mousehole. And Alan came rushing down from the reception and started to make us some drinks so we could talk in a civilized manner —"

Hall choked.

"Kay called him Mr. Jameson and said she would file suit for divorce in the morning. He'd never see a cent of the Spaulding money and by the time she got through with his reputation he couldn't get a job sweeping up the floor at the station. And Alan hit her. But not hard enough. He's not really a decisive man, you know." Hope sounded rather apologetic. "And then Kay laughed at him. She said he wouldn't dare kill her. She'd left a full report of his activities prepared by a private detective called Artur Antonelli with Martha. And she pulled out that damned spray and shot at Alan and that's when he was goaded to fury and he took the ice pick and really let her have it."

After a moment Hope went on. "I might have known that Alan would crack wide open, but in a way that paid off because everyone thought it was a collapse brought about by shock and grief. Well, I'd got rid of Antonelli and then there was Martha. Something was always going wrong. All I could figure was to get her to my apartment and then I'd be free to search hers. Women are better at that than men are as a rule. And then she found the key and came here. The joker in the pack if there ever was one."

She coughed. "And there was no end to the nightmare. It just went on and on. And then the candy — and that failed —"

I should have remembered that Alan would know my birth date. Kay had mentioned it once while I was still living in her house.

She was silent for a long time, lost in her thoughts. "Alan," she began.

Hall said, "Lambert may have been the best thing that ever happened to you, Hope, but, by God, you're the worst thing that ever happened to him. Without you he'd still be playing heavy roles in westerns and riding to his heart's content on the desert, palling up with his friend Scott Jameson, having some easy women now and then, and gambling away his earnings happily at Las Vegas. That would have suited him to a T.

"Instead of that, you built him to the point where he believed in the image you had created: the warm, genial guy who was everybody's friend. And because of you, he's going to spend the rest of his life looking through bars. The rest of his natural life. Rotting away. Hating your guts. And you'll never see him again from the time when you leave the courtroom. You understand that?"

This was a Hall I had never known and Hope whimpered with pain. Then she said, "Well, in a sense, I'm glad it's all over. I didn't think it would be so awful. All that blood. And then getting her down the stairs and into that car. Alan had to leave me and get back to the reception and there she was, lolling on the back seat where anyone could see her, and in the rearview mirror her eyes, wide open! And then I had to look up Antonelli's office and rush up there and get to him before the news came out. I went to his office just as he was leaving it and a man at the cigar stand spoke to him. I followed him to the subway and then — he screamed — and when the train touched him —" She shuddered.

In answer to a tap on the door Wilkins's attendant opened it and admitted a middle-aged woman who looked around and then stood leaning against the wall. Hope did not seem to notice her, lost in a world of her own, an inferno of her own making.

"This," Wilkins said, "is Mary McLeod. She will help you pack, Mrs. Bancroft."

Hope did not move until the woman touched her arm gently and firmly. She got to her feet, swaying. "My clothes are in my apartment. I didn't keep anything here but one change."

Wilkins nodded to the detective and he and the matron led Hope away, looking very small between them. I didn't think she cared what happened. From the time when Hall had told her what she had done to Alan and that he would hate her for it, she had in a way been a dead woman.

It was daybreak when Hall carried me down the stairs to my apartment and unlocked the door. "You go to bed," he instructed me, "and stay there all day. Wilkins promised that the police won't talk to you until tomorrow. I'll come around in the afternoon and see you have something to eat."

"Haven't you work of your own to do?"

" 'I have no precious time at all to spend,/ Nor services to do till you require,' " he quoted, and set me down gently on the bed. "Can you manage all right?"

I looked around, saw the bars on the window, bars through which Alan and Hope would look for the rest of their lives. "No! No! I can't stay here. I can't."

"Shall I take you back to Beekman Towers?"

"I left my clothes at Hope's apartment and I can't go to a hotel without any luggage."

"Then I'll make you up a bed on the couch," he said in a tone of resignation, "and sleep in here. A martyr, that's what I am. And don't raise your hopes and think I'm going to kiss you good night. You're too sleepy to appreciate it."

The last thing I had thought I would do that night was to laugh.